**THE RIFF SERIES**

# Rock Riffs for Guitar.

by Mark Michaels.

**Amsco Publications**
New York/London/Sydney

Book design by Margo Dittmer
Cover design by Pearce Marchbank
Cover photo by Rod Shone
Edited by Peter Pickow

International Standard Book Number: 0.8256.2171.2

*Exclusive Distributors:*
Music Sales Corporation
24 East 22nd Street, New York, NY 10010 USA
Music Sales Limited
8/9 Frith Street, London W1V 5TZ England
Music Sales Pty. Limited
120 Rothschild Street, Rosebery, Sydney, NSW 2018, Australia

Printed in the United States of America by
Vicks Lithograph and Printing Corporation

# CONTENTS

# INTRODUCTION

Welcome to the revised, enlarged edition of *Rock Riffs for Guitar*. You will notice that many new riffs have been added, all of them inspired by some of today's top groups. These include Men at Work, Dire Straits, Foreigner, Elvis Costello, the Cars, Steely Dan, Heart, Prince, Fleetwood Mac, Stray Cats, Queen, Steve Miller, and the Pretenders. I have also added new sections on sixteenth-note riffs, riffs using fourths and fifths, and diminished and chromatic riffs.

This book is intended for those of you who are already playing some guitar and can read basic rhythm patterns, up to and including dotted eighth notes and sixteenth-note triplets. Play each riff slowly at first, paying particular attention to picking, fingering, and accent notation. All of these riffs were written for electric guitar and sound best when played on one.

When you are able to play the riffs I have written, begin to mix them up—experiment!—and create your own. Play the riffs in all keys, up or down an octave, backwards, and so on. Try various licks as intros, fills, solos, and endings to tunes you already know. Playing with another guitarist is an excellent way to develop your musical skills; another way is to practice with a metronome and still another is to tape yourself playing rhythm and then play along to the tape.

The references which accompany the riffs direct your attention to popular songs and performers who have used—or might use—riffs similar to the ones in this book. I have included a full discography at the end of the book which further directs you to specific albums by artists featuring notable guitarists; you should try to listen to as many of them as possible.

In order to fully benefit from the material presented in *Rock Riffs for Guitar*, you may order a cassette of all of the riffs herein. There is nothing like actually hearing what you are going to be playing. At the end of the book, you will find information regarding this cassette, the *Rock Riff Companion*.

Good luck and keep practicin'!

MARK MICHAELS

# SYMBOLS AND NOTATION

|  |  |
|---|---|
| ⊓ | downstroke |
| V | upstroke |
| > | accent |
| ⌇⌇⌇ | heavy vibrato |
| ⟋ | slide up |
| ⟍ | slide down |
| ♩ | harmonic (notation) |
| ♦ | harmonic (tablature) |
| tr | trill |
| PO | pulloff |
| H | hammeron |
| BU | bend up |
| BD | bend down |
| SL | slide |
| PSL | pick, then slide |
| SLP | slide, then pick |
| ML | mute with left hand |
| MR | mute with right hand |
| MLR | mute with left and right hands |
| R | fret with right-hand finger |
| 8va | play an octave higher than written |

When notes are written inside parentheses, they are to be fingered but not played. I use this notation to show which fret to finger when bending notes. Notes that are not to be bent but are also within parentheses are ghost notes, which may or may not be played.

## Developing a Riff: Bending, Hammering On, and Pulling Off

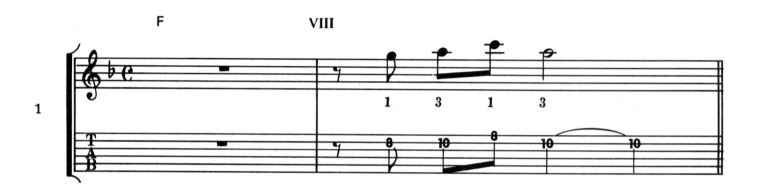

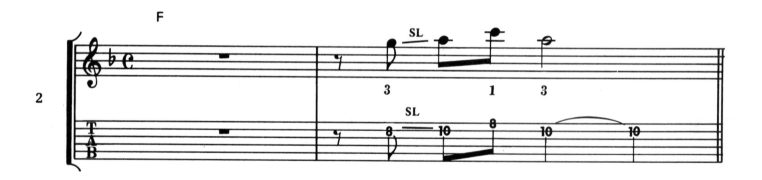

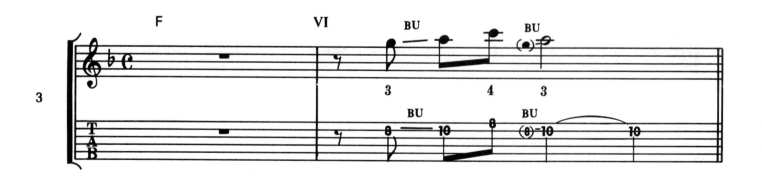

The following four riffs are similar to those played by Mick Ralphs in Bad Company's "Deal with the Preacher."

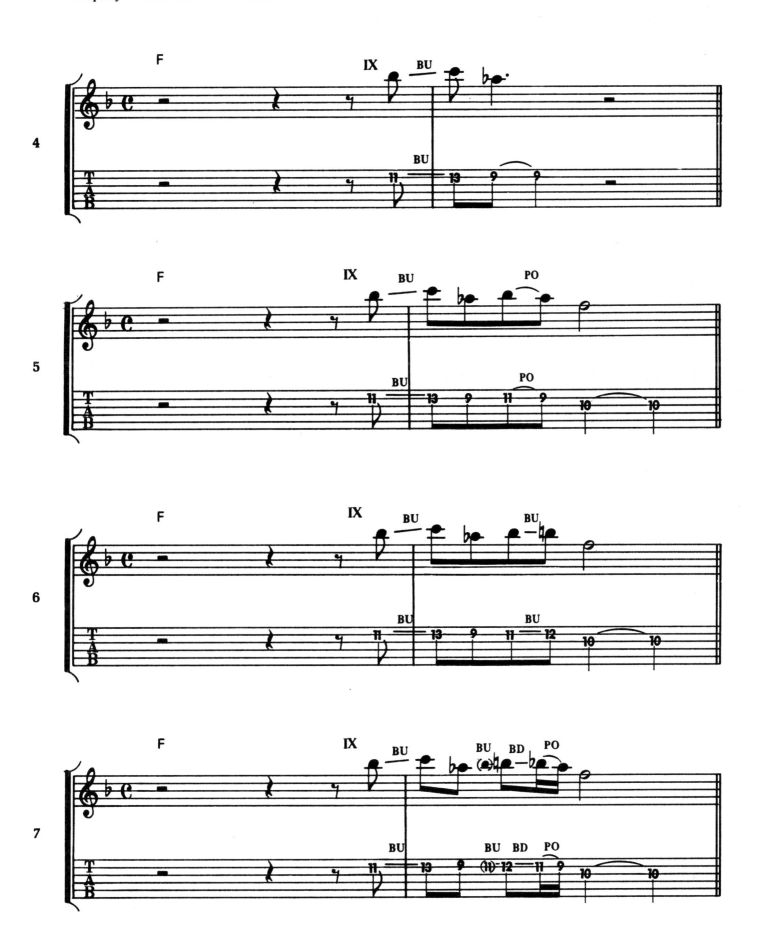

Listen to "Mississippi Queen" by Leslie West of Mountain to hear a riff similar to this one.

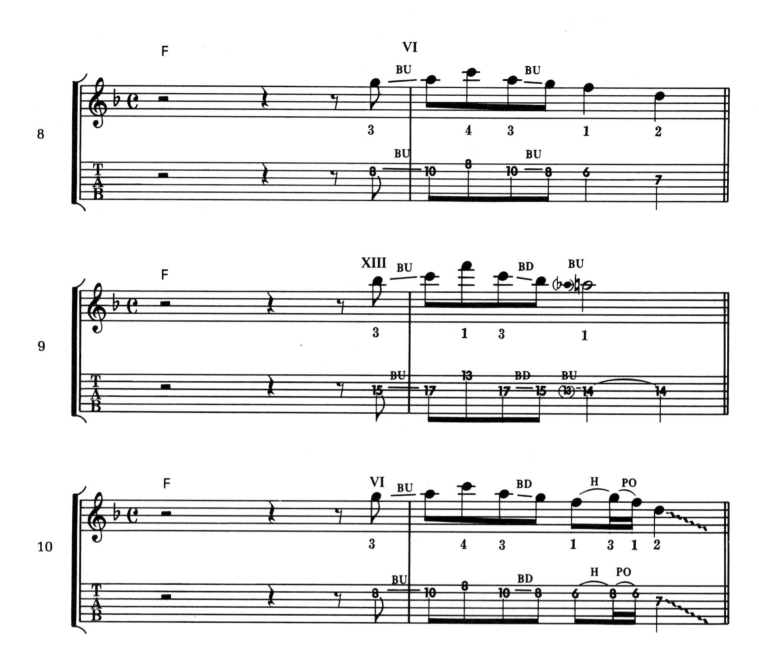

This is a basic blues-rock riff based on the playing of Albert King. You'll hear it often in the playing of Eric Clapton and Peter Green.

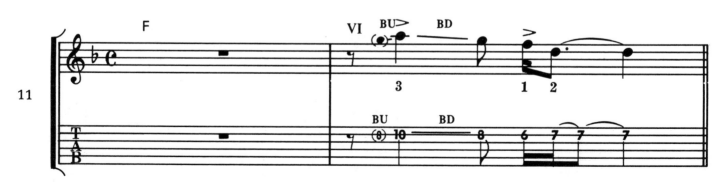

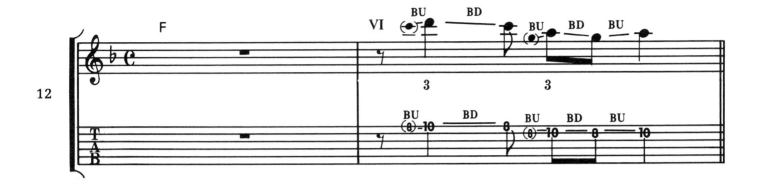

# Developing a Riff: Expanding on a Theme

Brian May of Queen develops a riff like this one nicely in "Great King Rat."

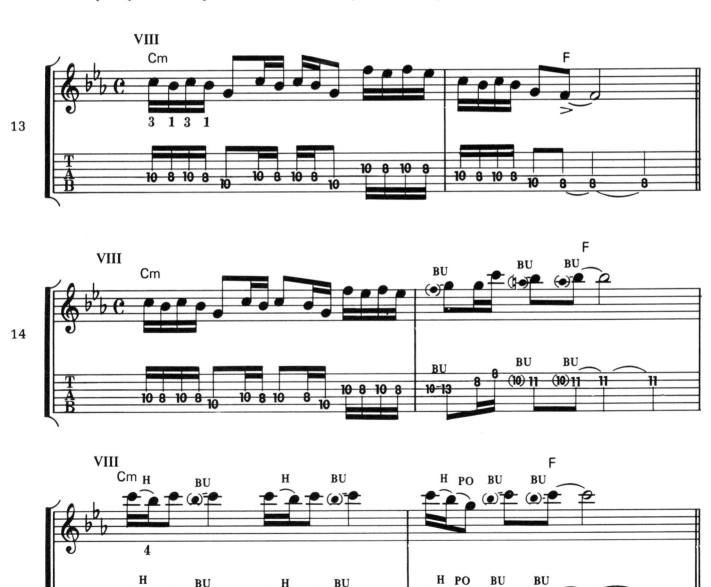

Lindsay Buckingham develops a riff with a similar motif in the introduction (and later the solo) to "You Make Loving Fun."

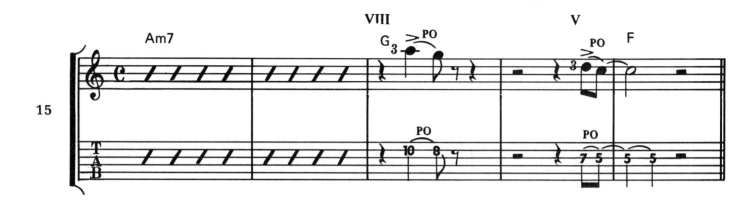

# Single-Note Riffs: One Measure Long

The following riff is typical of the style of Mick Ralphs of Bad Company (listen to their "Can't Get Enough"). Notice the E against the B♭ chord, which is a ♭5.

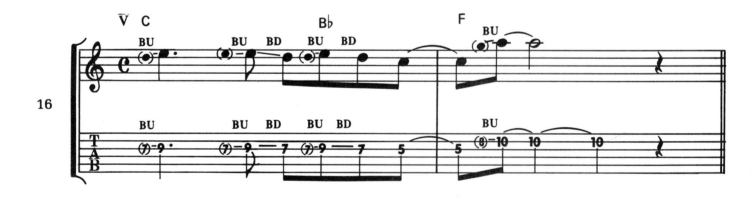

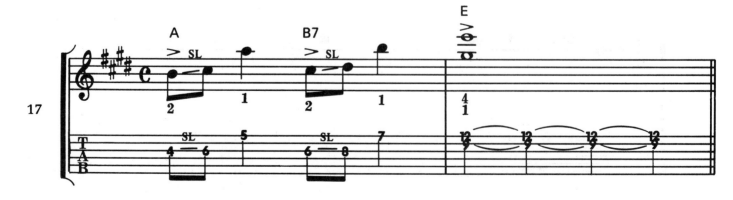

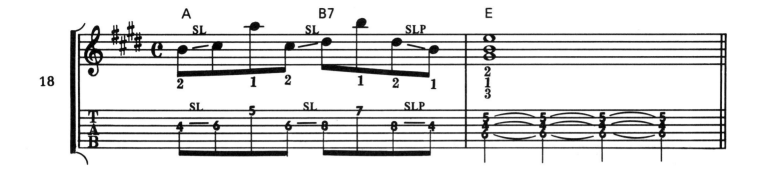

Listen to the intro to Foreigner's "Woman in Black" to hear something like this. Note that the D♯ note is diatonic to the key of E (the C♯m chord is the VI chord in E).

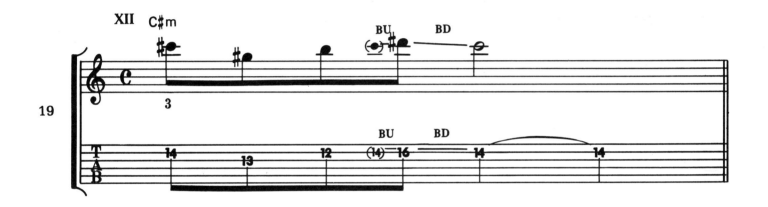

Duane Allman plays like this on "Ramblin' Man" and "Sweet Melissa."

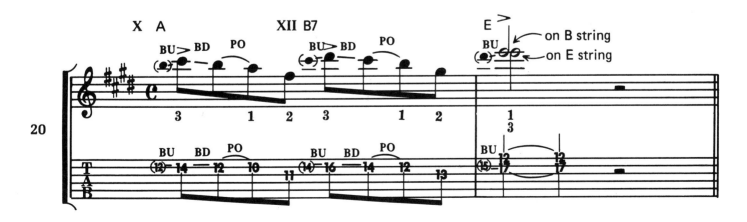

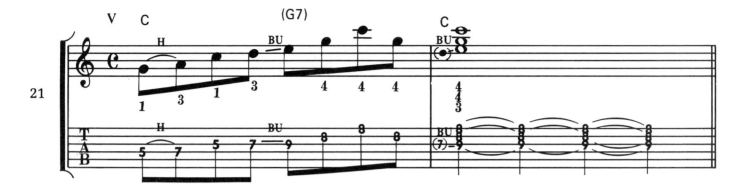

Listen to Bo Diddley, Chuck Berry, and the Monkees' "I'm a Believer."
Then play this.

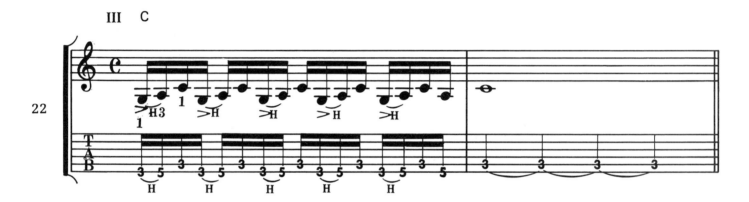

This blues-rock lick ends on the sixth note (F♯) of the A Major scale, a
strong interval.

George Harrison plays a riff similar to the one below on the Beatles'
"Another Girl" from the *Help!* album.

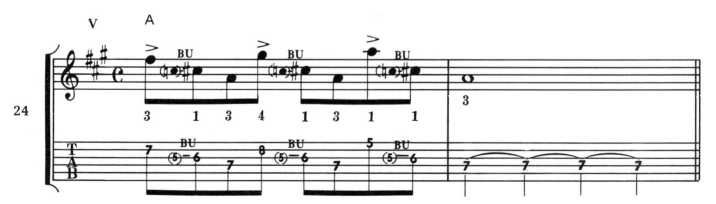

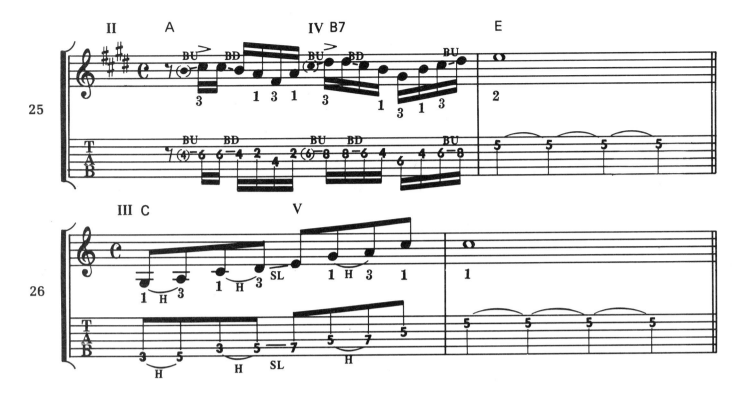

The following riff mimics a pedal steel guitar. Listen to the playing of Jerry Corbitt, Clarence White, and Cornell Dupree.

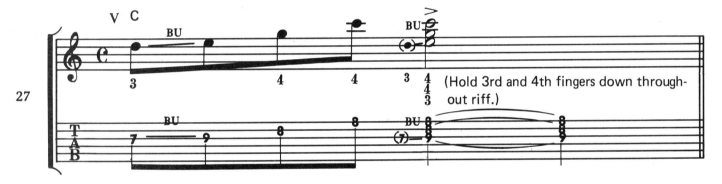

# Single-Note Riffs: Two Measures Long

You'll hear Mark Knopfler play a riff similar to the following one on Dire Straits' "Sultans of Swing."

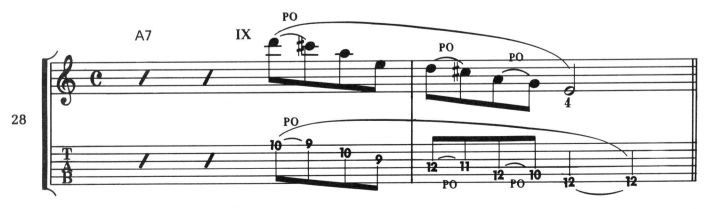

Dave Edmunds plays a riff like this one in his solo on "Crawling from the Wreckage," on his album *Repeat When Necessary*.

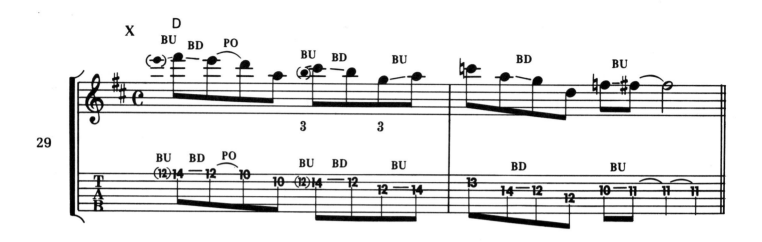

Although a riff like the following is played on slide guitar in Elvis Costello's "Waitin' for the End of the World," it is easily adapted to flat-picking.

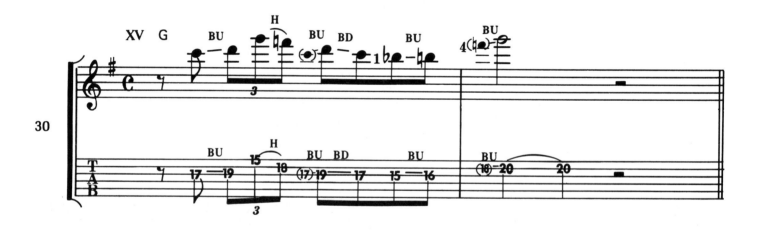

Jerry Reed or Glen Campbell might play something like this.

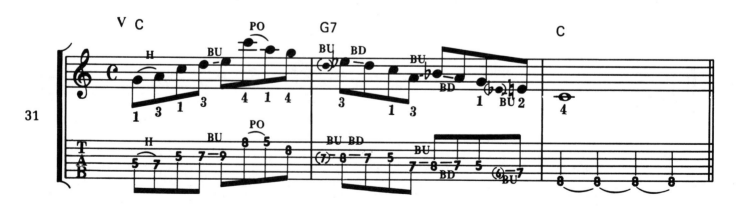

Mick Ralphs of Bad Company plays something like the following riff in their song "Good Lovin' Gone Bad."

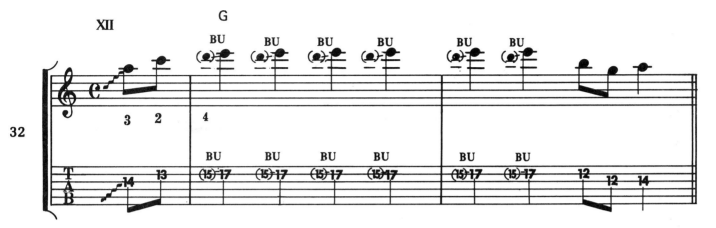

This riff is played off the blues (box) fingering. Listen to Bad Company's "Shooting Star" on their first album.

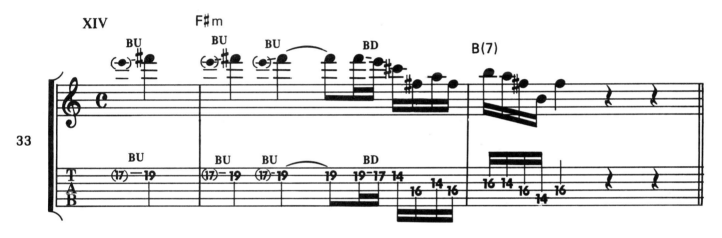

Introducing a bluesy element (♭3) à la Albert King.

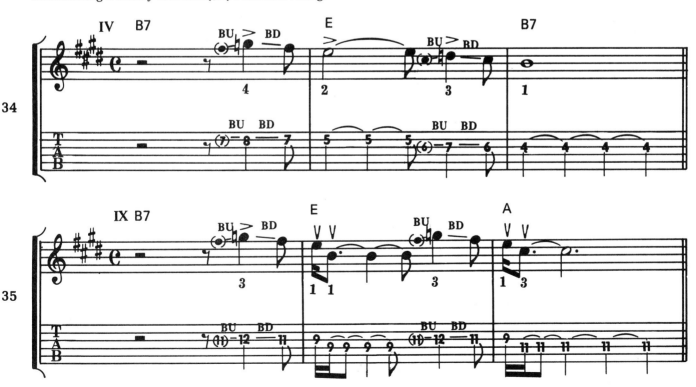

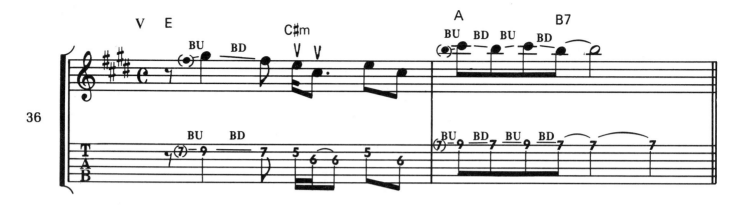

This riff resembles what Prince plays in his song "Little Red Corvette."

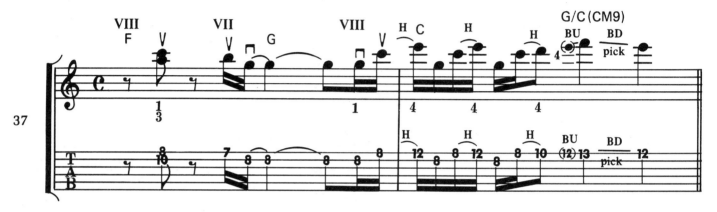

Listen to the Cars' "You Can't Hold on Too Long" to hear a riff similar to this one. The correct key signature for B Major is in parentheses, for your knowledge, although the riff is notated in C (no sharps, no flats).

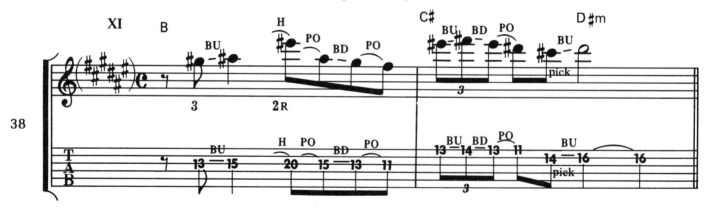

You can hear a riff similar to this bluesy riff played by the Cars' Elliot Easton in their song "Got a Lot on My Head."

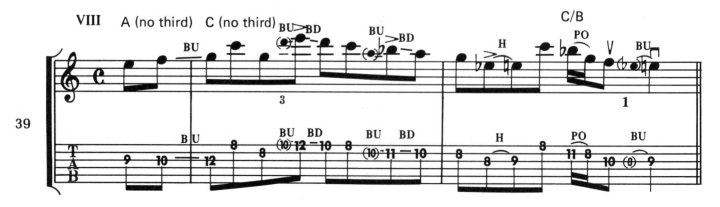

Listen to Bad Company's "Deal with the Preacher" to hear a riff similar to this one.

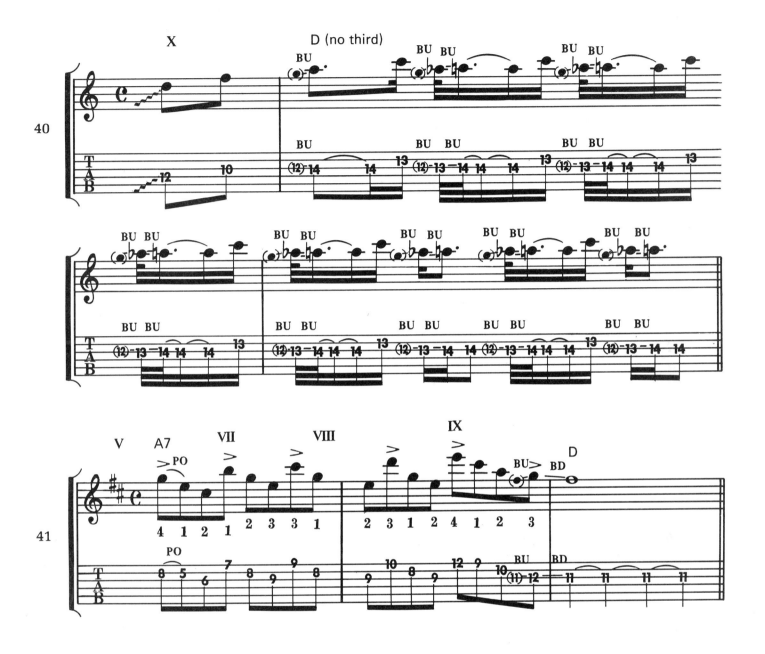

Steve Cropper uses riffs like this one.

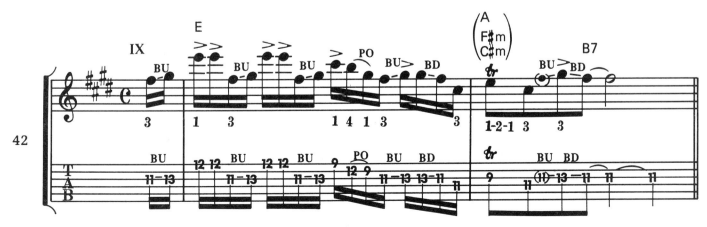

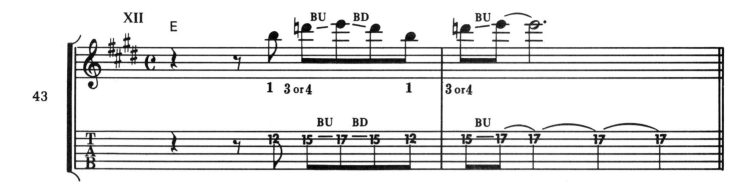

Listen to Jeff Beck's *Truth* and *Beck-Ola* to hear this kind of riff.

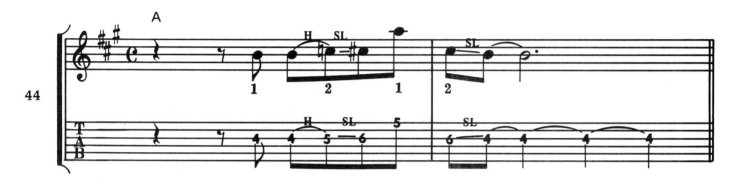

This can also be played against E-C♯m-A-B7-E.

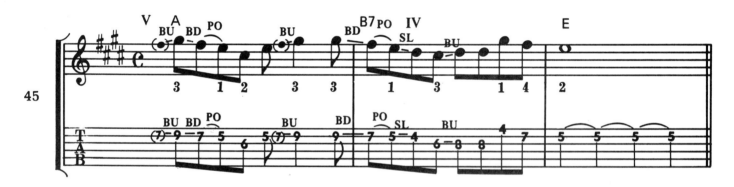

# Single-Note Riffs: Three or More Measures Long

The late James Honeyman-Scott played something similar to this riff in the Pretenders' "Kid."

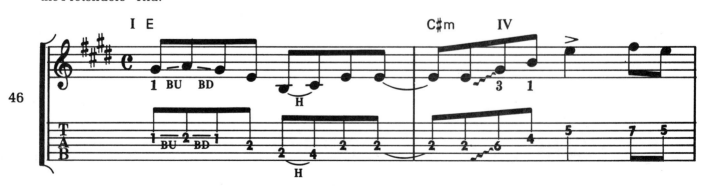

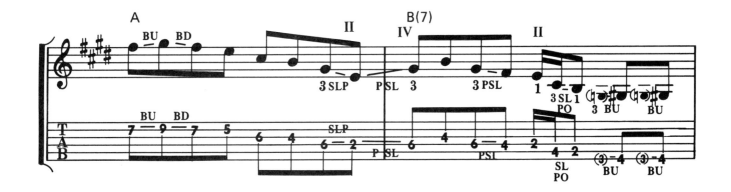

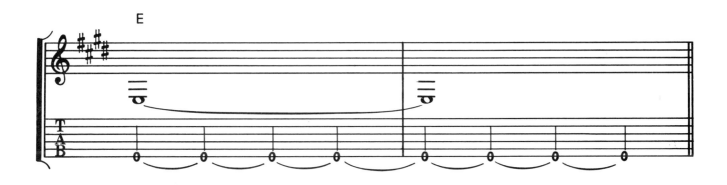

Here's another riff similar to what Scott played with the Pretenders.

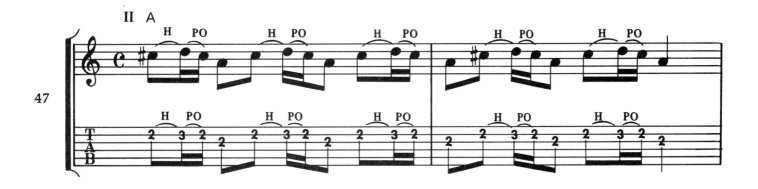

47

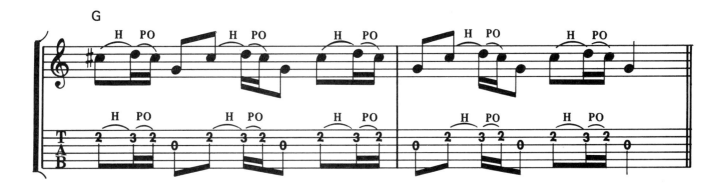

Listen to "Bad Sneakers" on Steely Dan's *Katy Lied* album to hear a riff like this one. The song has a half-time (slow four) feel to it.

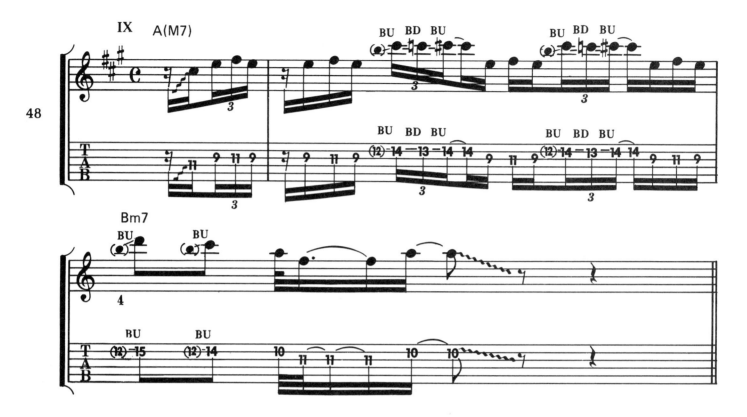

Listen to Fleetwood Mac's "I Think I'm in Trouble" to hear a riff approximating the following.

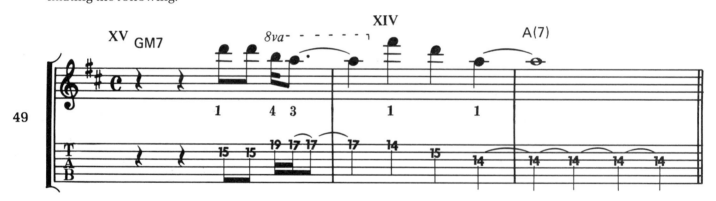

For sounds similar to this, listen to "Station Man" on Fleetwood Mac's album *Kiln House* and to "Octopus' Garden" on the Beatles' *Abbey Road*.

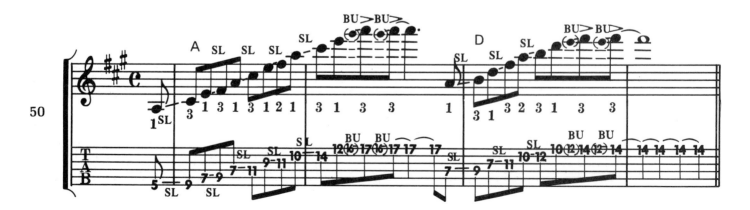

This riff combines elements of Jerry Reed's and Albert King's styles.

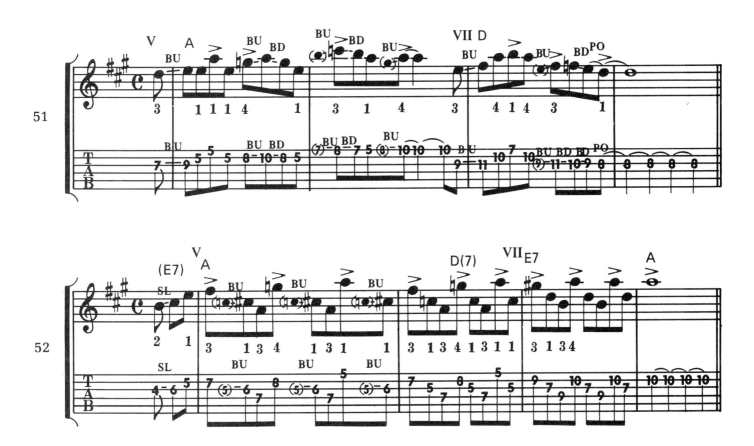

Mick Ronson plays a riff resembling this one in Ian Hunter's "Cleveland Rocks."

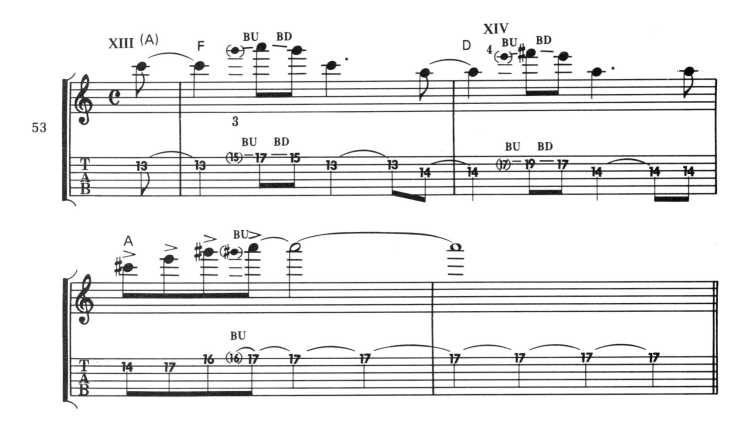

This very melodic riff is similar to what Mick Ronson plays on David Bowie's "Hang on to Yourself."

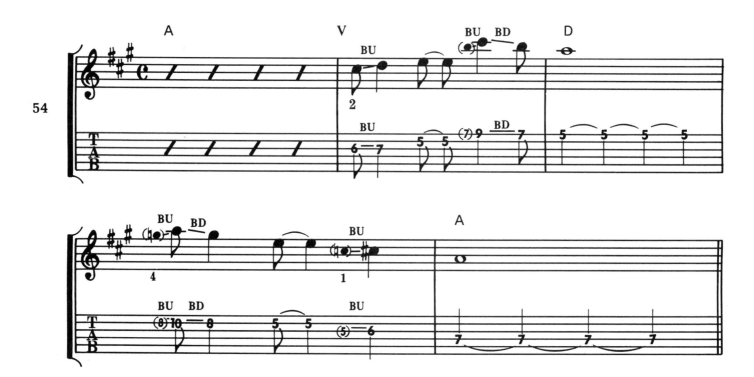

Listen to Dire Straits' "Sultans of Swing" to hear Mark Knopfler play a riff like this one.

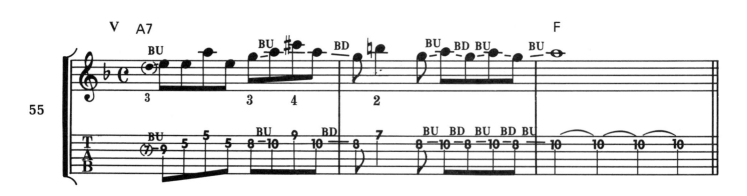

The riff below is similar to the one in Freddie King's "Hideaway," a rock classic.

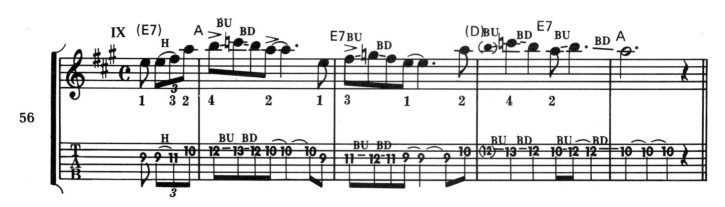

# Triplet Riffs: Alternate Picking

This riff is similar to what Mick Ralphs plays in Bad Company's "Can't Get Enough." The high E♭ is in the blues scale of C and against the G7 acts as a ♯5.

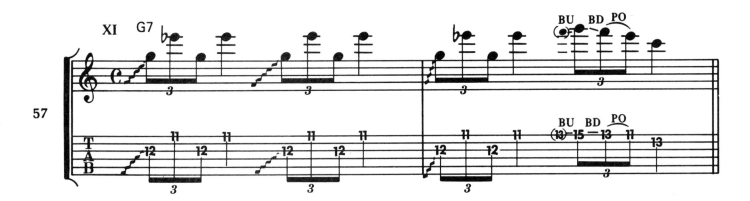

This quarter-note triplet riff, played against a shuffle rhythm, makes use of the second and sixth intervals in the A Major scale. Listen to Mick Ronson's playing with Ian Hunter.

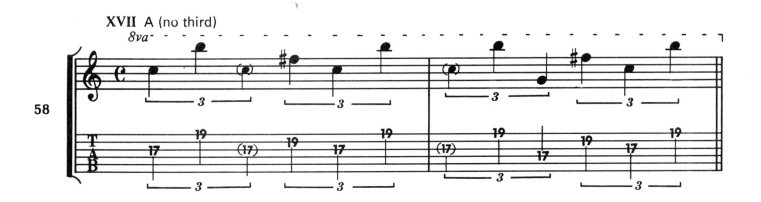

This riff produces a drone; check out the playing of Jimmy Page and of Jeff Beck with the Yardbirds for similar effects.

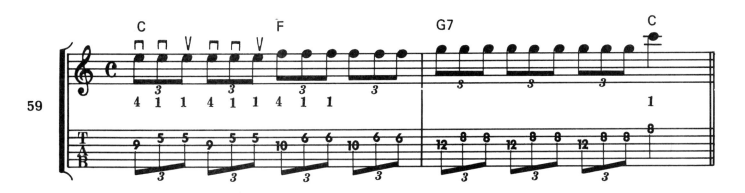

Listen to "Beck's Boogie" on the Yardbirds' album *Over, Under, Sideways, Down*, the Stones' "Let the Good Times Roll," and the Beatles' "You Really Got a Hold on Me." Then play this.

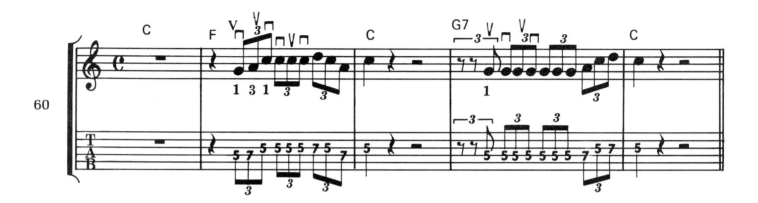

# Triplet Riffs: Hammering On

This is a Chuck Berry / Bo Diddley type rock riff.

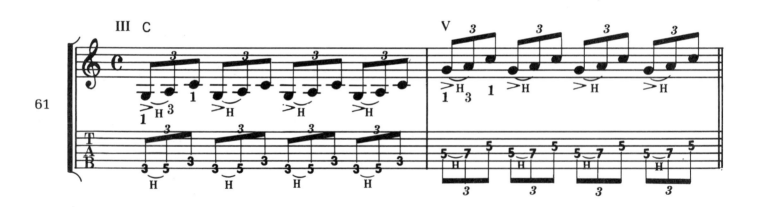

Keith Richard plays a riff like this on the Rolling Stones' "Rockin' an' Reelin'."

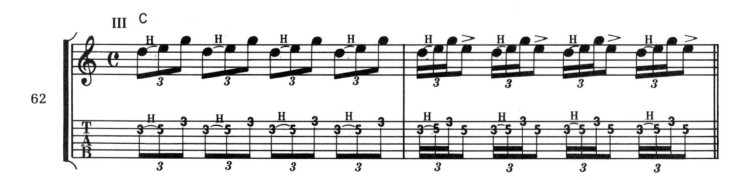

# Triplet Riffs: Bending

This traditional rock and roll riff is close to what Brian Setzer plays in "Stray Cat Strut."

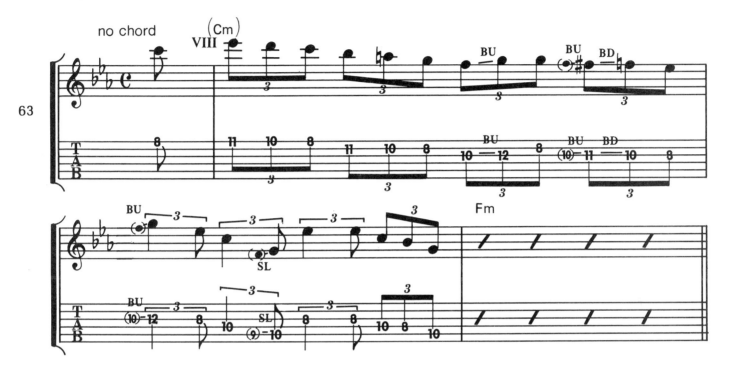

You'll hear a riff similar to the following one in Heart's "Mistral Wind."

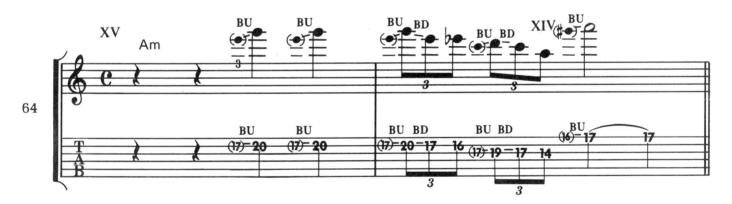

While holding the pick as usual, your middle and ring fingers are still free to pick notes upward, giving a unique sound to this riff. Listen to Steely Dan's "Black Friday."

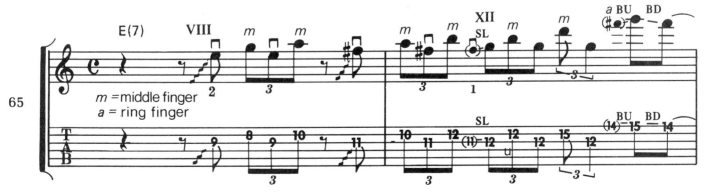

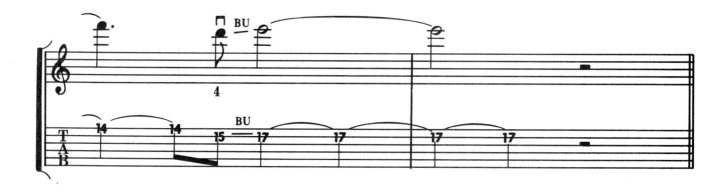

The following riff combines ideas from the playing of George Harrison and Steve Cropper.

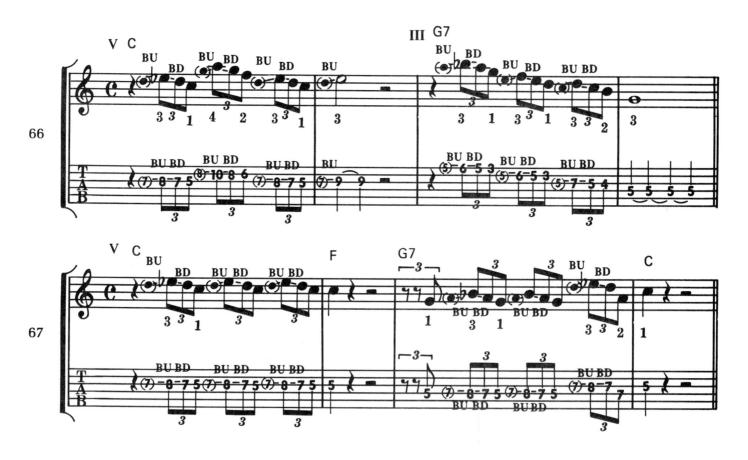

Listen to Mick Jones's solo in Foreigner's "I Need You" to hear a riff like this one.

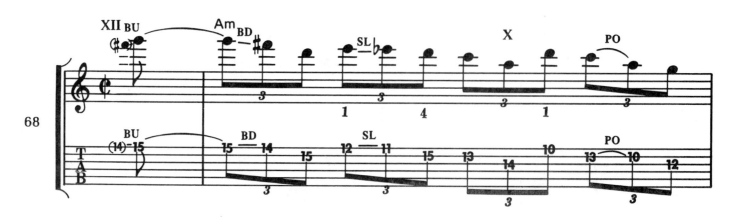

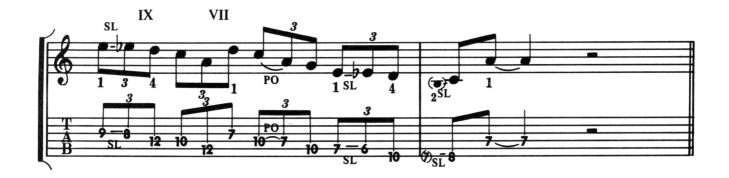

Robbie Robertson of the Band plays phrases like this one.

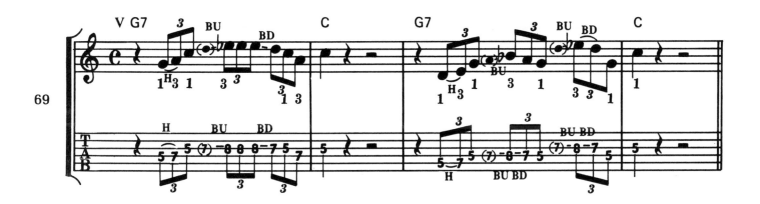

# Triplet Riffs: Pulling Off

This unusual riff (you'll hear one just like it in Heart's "Mistral Wind")
features a pulloff to the (open) B string.

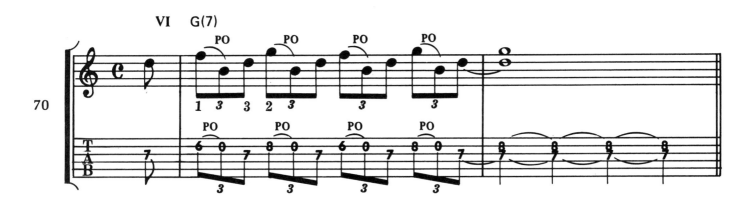

# Sixteenth-Note Riffs

This riff, using the notes from the F Major scale, is a neat way to go from the VI chord to the IV, and then to the V7. Lindsay Buckingham plays something similar in "Who Wrote the Book of Love."

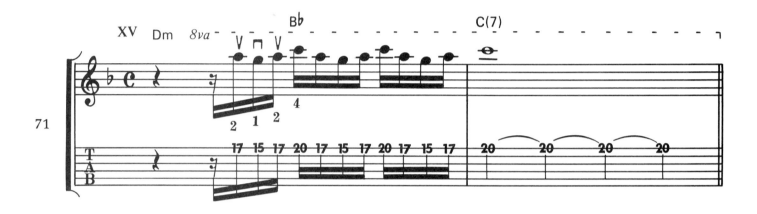

You'll hear a riff resembling this one in the Pretenders' "Every Day."

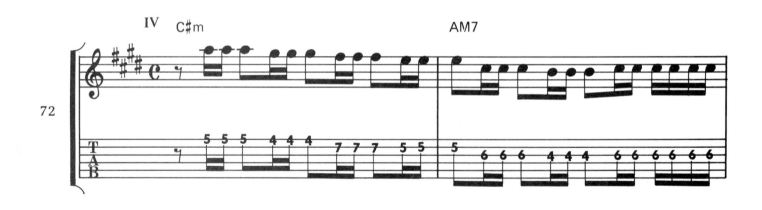

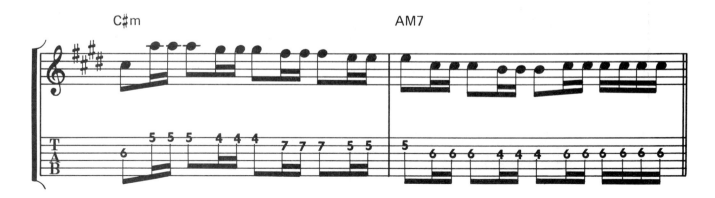

Check out Dire Straits' "Down to the Waterline" to hear a riff similar to the following one. It's played off the regular blues (box) fingering pattern.

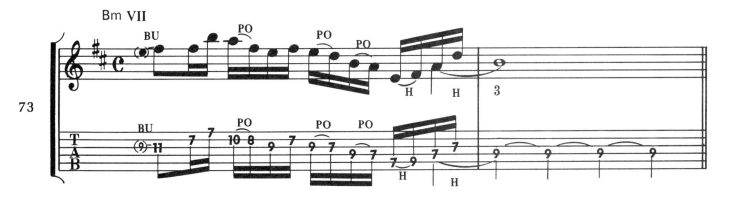

Listen to the intro to Savoy Brown's "Oo What a Feeling" (on *Wirefire*) to hear a riff like this one.

Listen to Clapton's "Keep On Growin'" and the entire *Layla* album to hear these kinds of bluesy country licks.

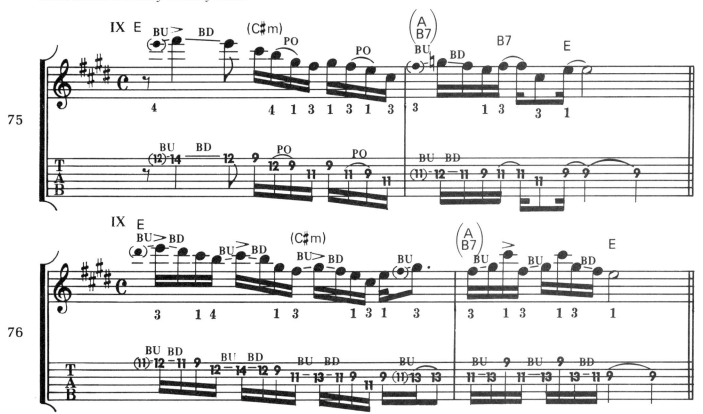

# Sixteenth-Note Riffs: Pulling Off

This riff just looks difficult; start slowly and soon you'll have it mastered.
Listen to the tag on "Sultans of Swing" to hear something like it.

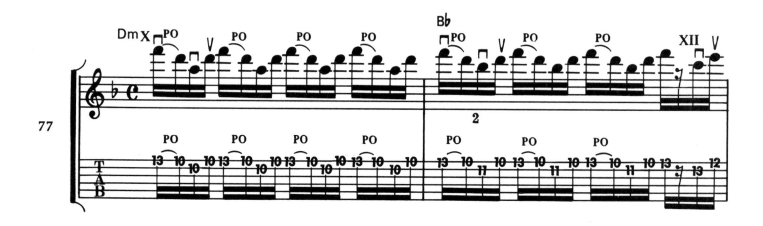

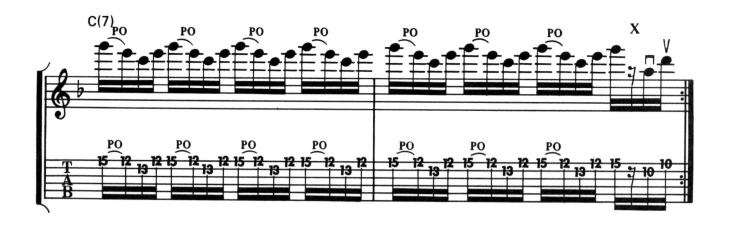

A riff similar to this one can be heard in Heart's "Mistral Wind." See the section "Triplet Riffs: Pulling Off" for a riff like this one using triplets instead of sixteenth notes.

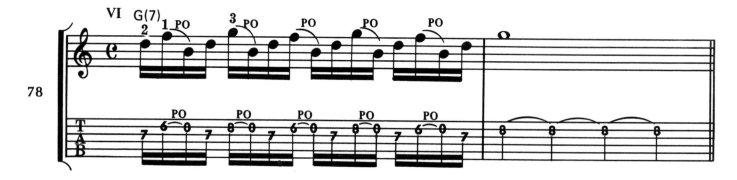

The B note held through all three chords here is dissonant against the F chord (it's the ♭5) but consonant against the G chord. Listen to Mick Ronson on Bowie's *Ziggy Stardust* album.

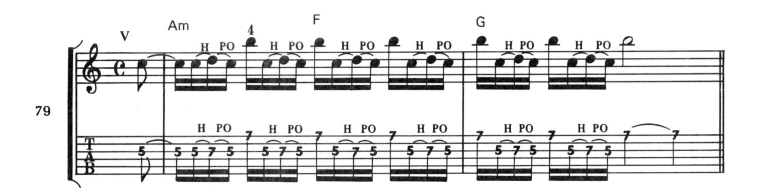

You'll hear a riff similar to the following one in Heart's "Crazy on You." Watch the fourth finger stretch on the third beat.

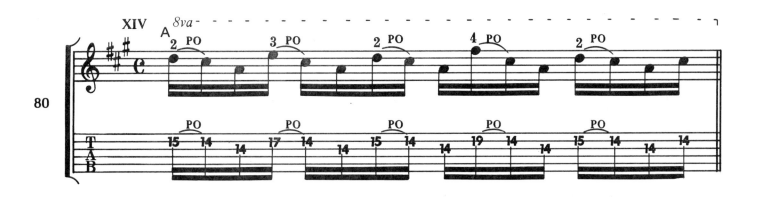

You can hear a riff like the following played by Brian May in Queen's "Great King Rat."

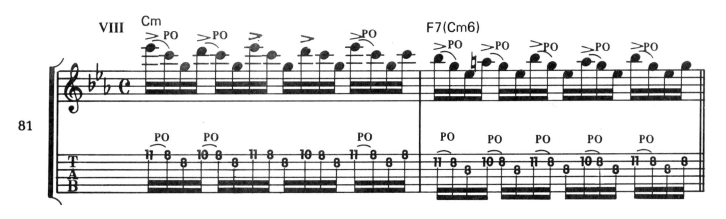

# Left-Hand Muting

To mute with the left hand, finger the note but don't press down all the way on the string.

Accenting a different note in each beat of the first measure of this riff is a very ear-catching device. Listen to Fleetwood Mac's "You Make Loving Fun."

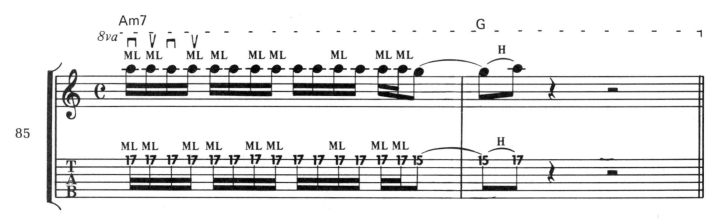

Listen to Steely Dan's "My Old School" and "Friday on My Mind" by the Easybeats (also David Bowie on *Pinups*) to hear riffs like these.

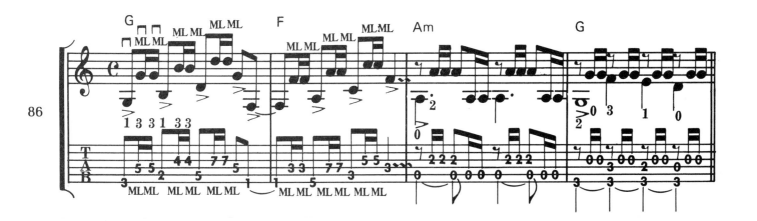

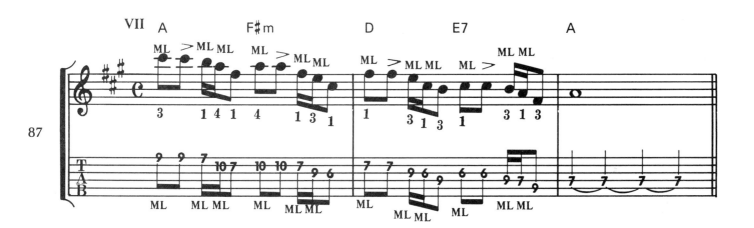

Muting a note automatically accents the following note.

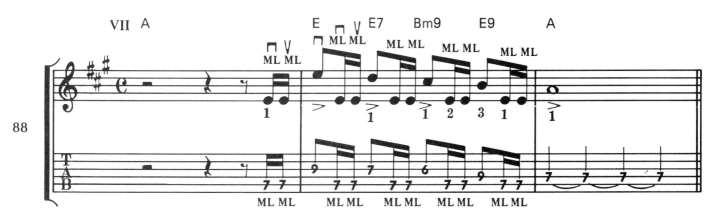

## Muting and Bending

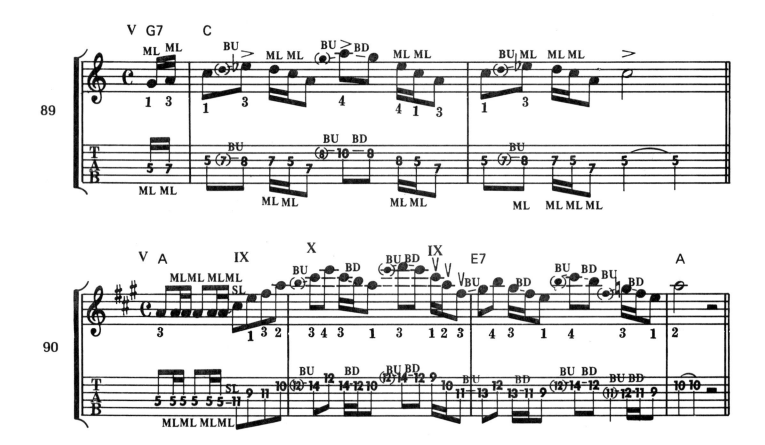

## Muted Chordal Riffs

The symbol x indicates a completely muted note. This riff is used a lot by Boston ("Long Time") and Steve Miller ("Lost in Space," "Take the Money and Run").

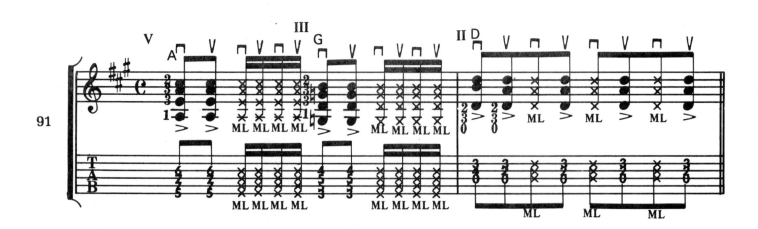

Listen to the Young Rascals' "C'mon Up" and Sam and Dave's "You Got Me Hummin."

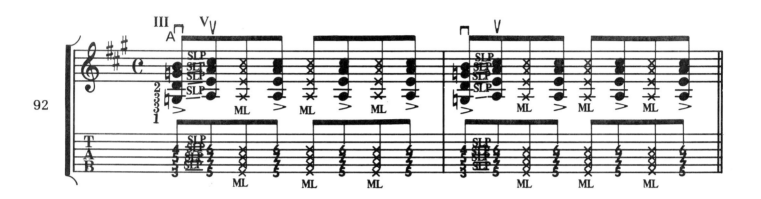

This kind of riff is used by the Kinks on "You Really Got Me" and "All Day and All of the Night."

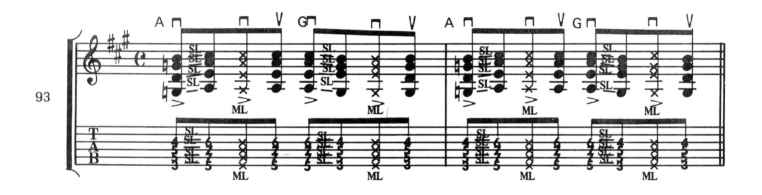

Listen to the Stones' "Honky-Tonk Women."

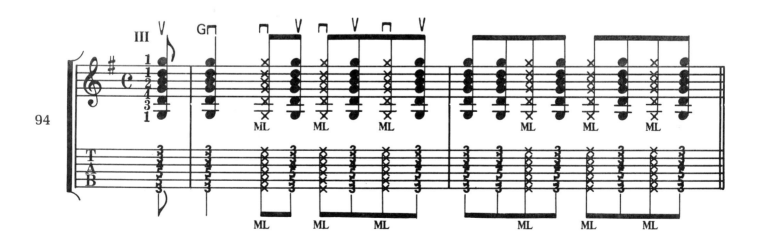

# Descending-Bass Riffs

Bad Company's "Deal with the Preacher" features a riff like this one. The E natural against the last chord is a strong interval.

The next two riffs can be heard in similar form in Bad Company's "Call on Me." In the second riff, the F Major scale is appropriate as Gm/E is equivalent to C9 (C7), the V7 chord in the key of F.

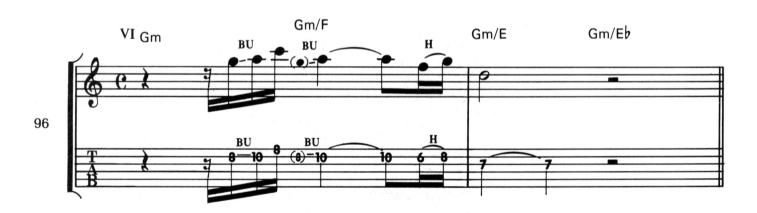

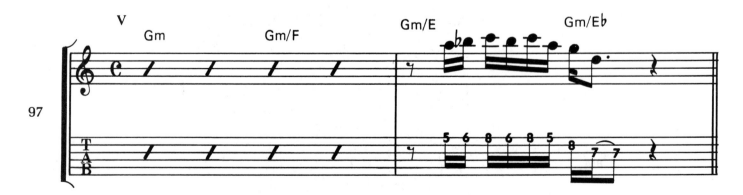

This riff is similar to what George plays on "While My Guitar Gently Weeps" (the Beatles' *White Album*).

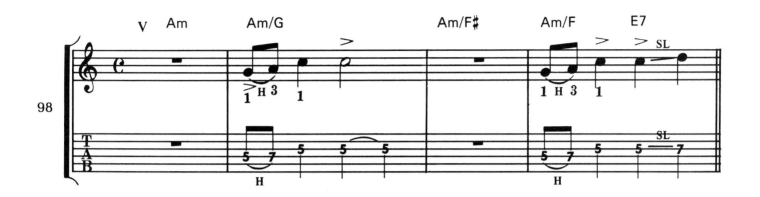

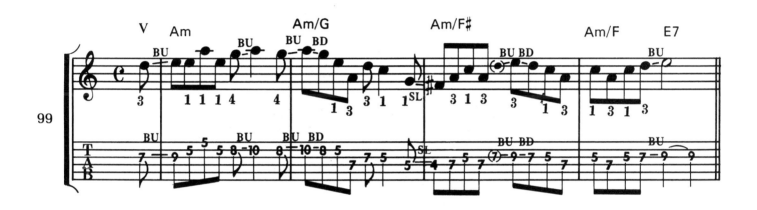

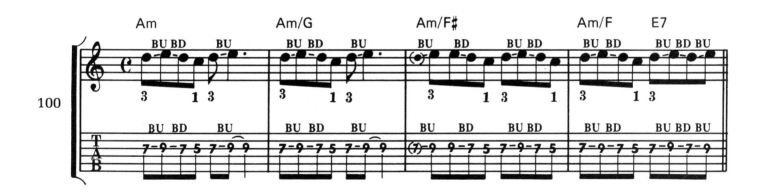

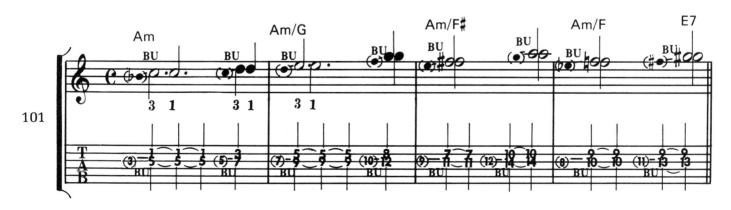

Listen to Eric Clapton's playing on John Mayall's *Bluesbreakers* album.

# Double-Note Riffs: Alternate Strings

Listen to Van Morrison's "Brown-Eyed Girl."

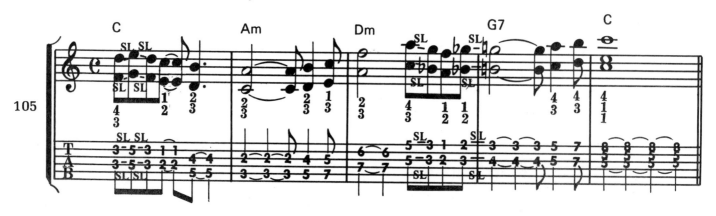

Cornell Dupree might play something like this on "Mercy, Mercy."

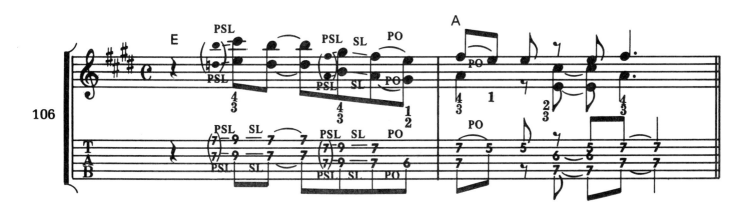

"And Your Bird Can Sing" on the Beatles' *Yesterday and Today* is reminiscent of these riffs — a semiclassical feel.

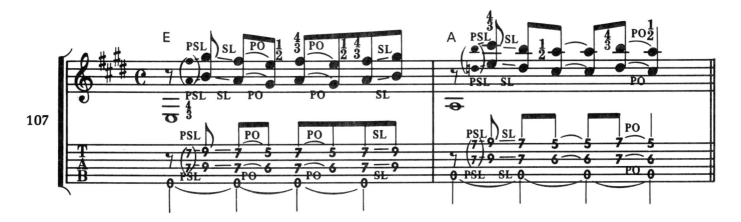

# Double-Note Riffs: Adjacent Strings

This riff is similar to what Mick Jones plays in his solo in Foreigner's "Woman in Black."

These are country-blues riffs that sound good with rock and roll pro-
gressions. They come from players like Mississippi John Hurt, Carl
Perkins, and James Burton.

Jimi Hendrix often played riffs like this one. Listen especially to "All Along the Watchtower."

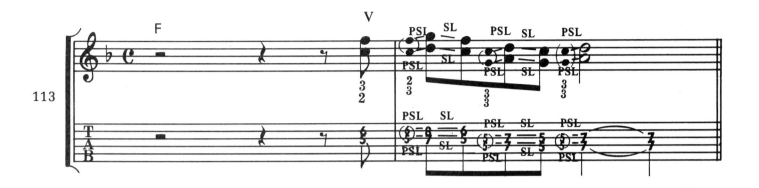

These riffs are written in the style of Cornell Dupree and Steve Cropper. Listen to Brook Benton's "Rainy Night in Georgia."

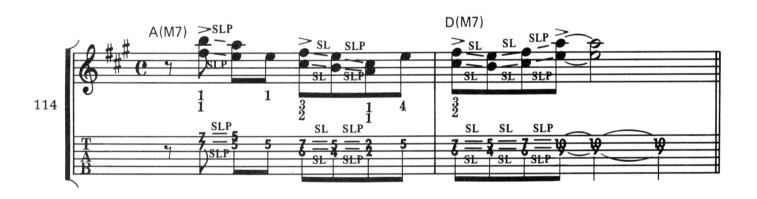

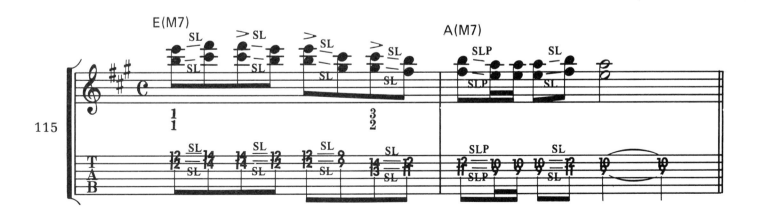

# Double-Note Riffs: Adjacent Strings with Hammering On and Pulling Off

Listen to Elvis Costello's "Miracle Man" to hear a riff like this one.

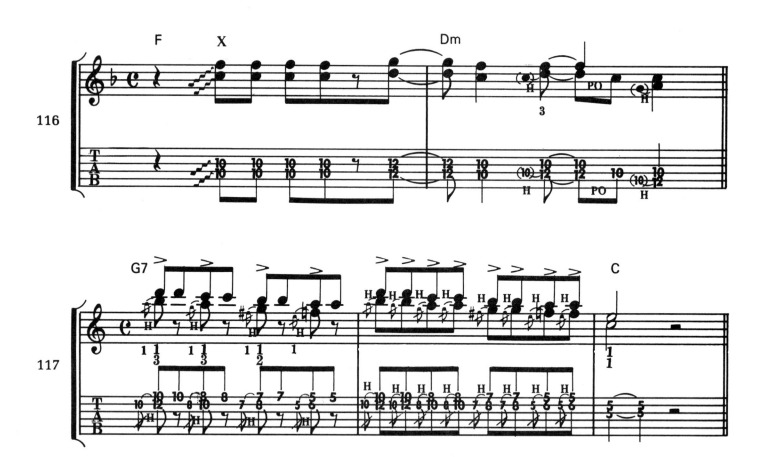

Listen to Michael Bloomfield with the Paul Butterfield Blues Band for other riffs like this one.

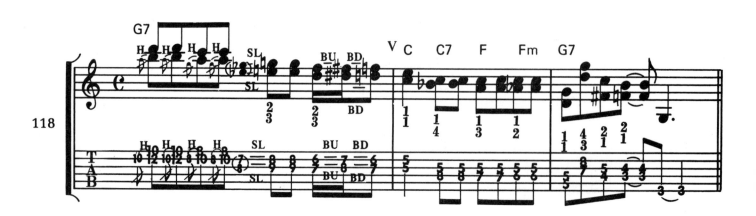

The Eagles' guitarist plays riffs like this in the tune "Hotel California."

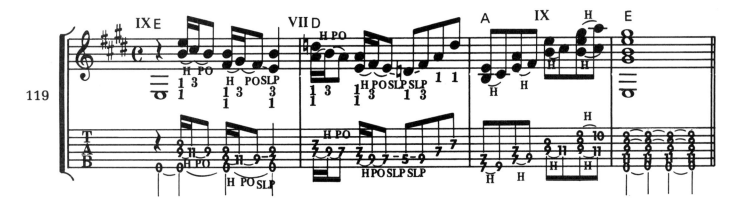

This is one of Hendrix's characteristic riffs, heard in "Little Wing," "The Wind Cries Mary," "Castles Made of Sand," and others. Also listen to the Stones' "Moonlight Mile."

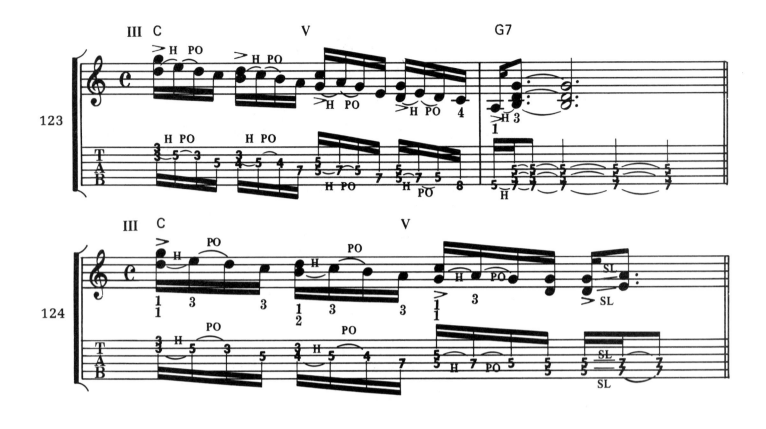

# Double-Note Riffs: Adjacent Strings with Bending

A riff like this one is played as a fill by Brian Setzer in the Stray Cats' "Stray Cat Strut." Note the use of both the ♯5 and ♭5 in the second measure.

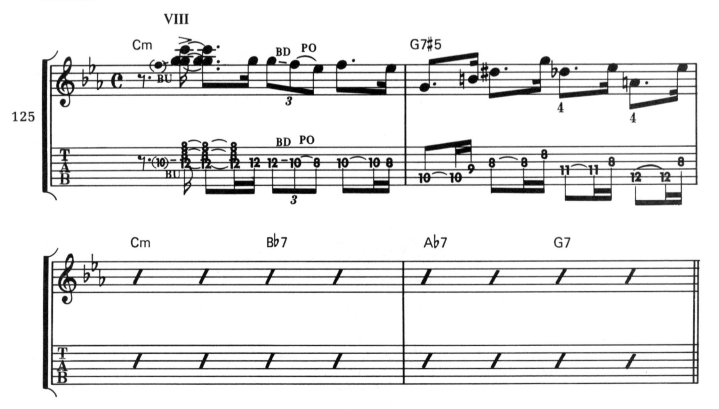

Listen to Bad Company's "Good Lovin' Gone Bad" to hear something like the following riff.

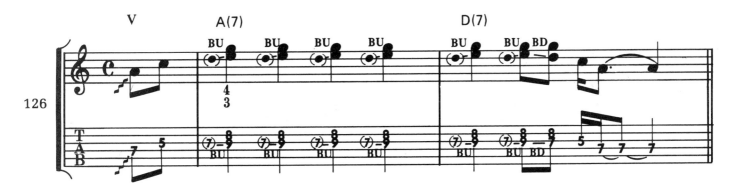

Jimi Hendrix used this technique a lot.

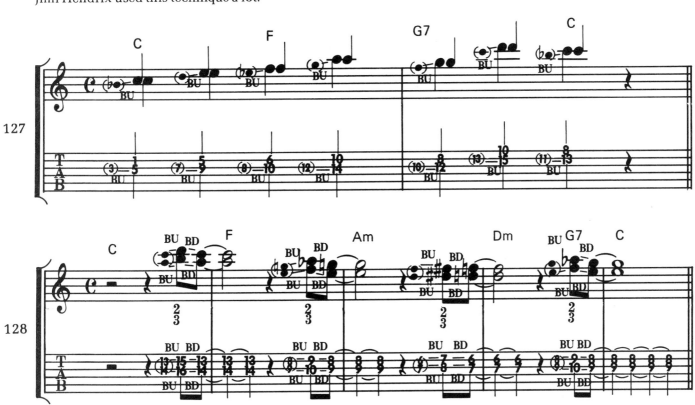

Play this riff against "Layla" on the *Derek and the Dominoes* (Allman and Clapton) album.

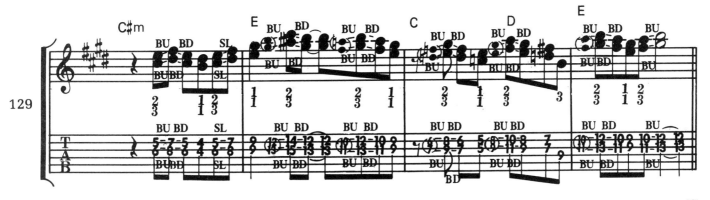

# Right-Hand Muting

Rest palm of right hand lightly just before the bridge on string to be muted.

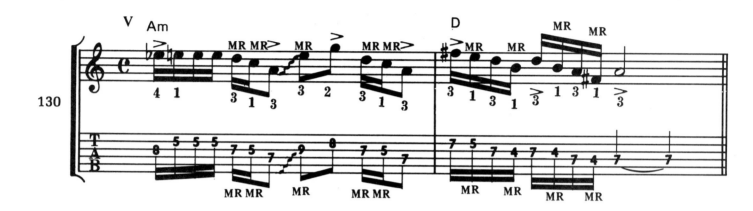

See "Whole Lotta Love" by Led Zeppelin (Jimmy Page).

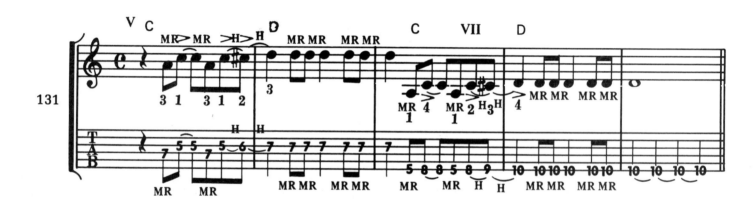

Listen to Bob Marley's "No Woman No Cry" to hear this reggae-like deadening effect.

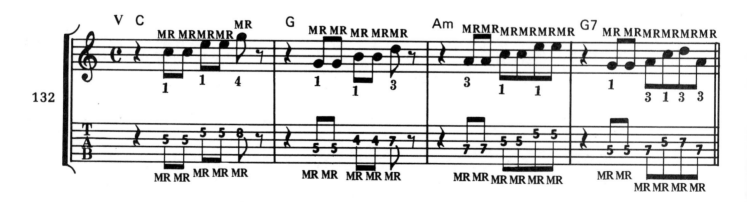

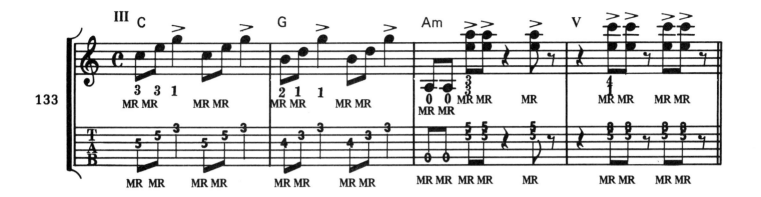

# Left- and Right-Hand Muting

This next riff is similar to the one the Eagles use in the opening to "One of These Nights." Right- and left-hand muting provide a very dead sound.

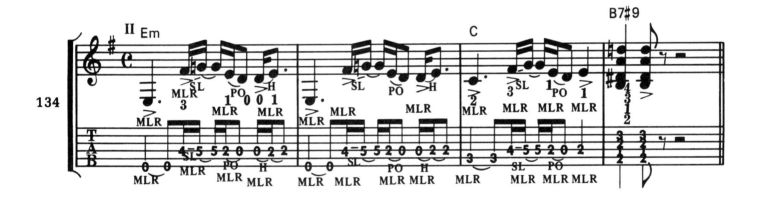

Hold your right palm down throughout this riff.

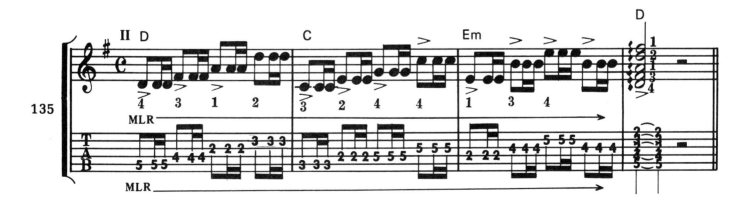

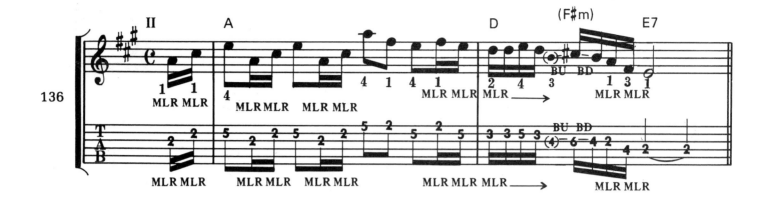

Sound familiar? (The "William Tell Overture")

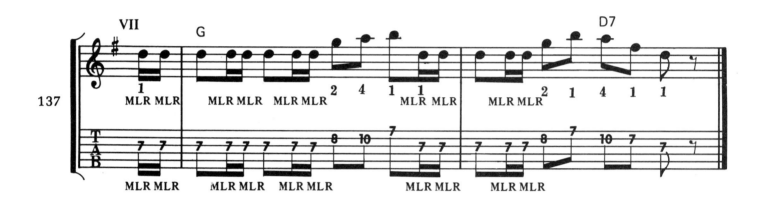

# Riffs Using Fourths and Fifths

Mark Knopfler of Dire Straits plays a riff resembling this one.

Check out the end of Steely Dan's "Black Friday" to hear something like the following riff. The cycle of fourths starts on the last note (D) of the second measure.

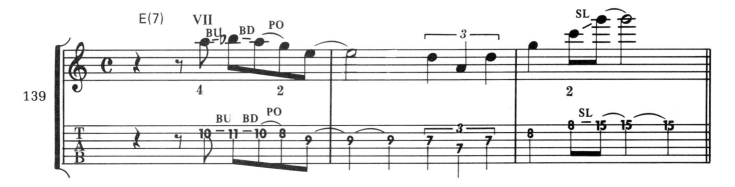

When the initial motif here is repeated against the D chord, the G♯ (diatonic to the key of A) becomes a ♭5. Listen to Fleetwood Mac's "Can't Go Back" and use your chorus effect.

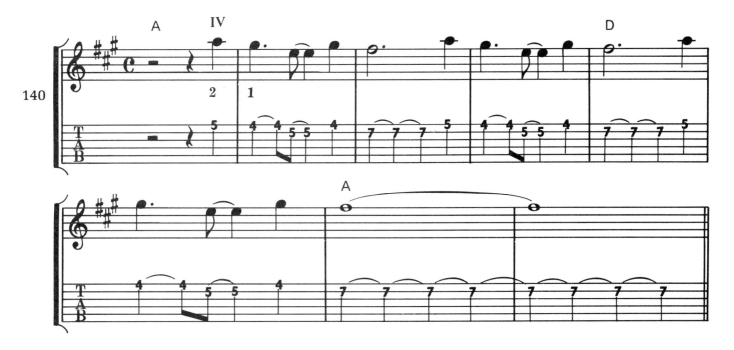

In this riff, the notes of a Dmaj6 chord (the equivalent of a Bm, the II chord in the key of A) are played against an A chord. See Men at Work's "I Like To."

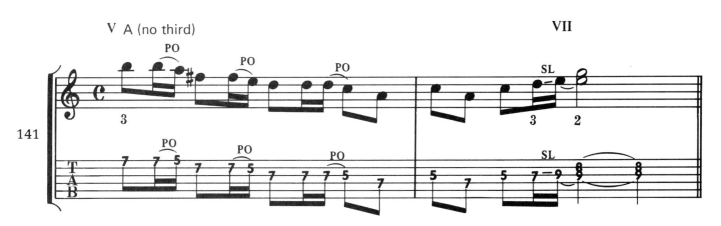

Mick Ronson plays a harmonic fill resembling this one on "Ziggy Stardust" from David Bowie's album of the same name.

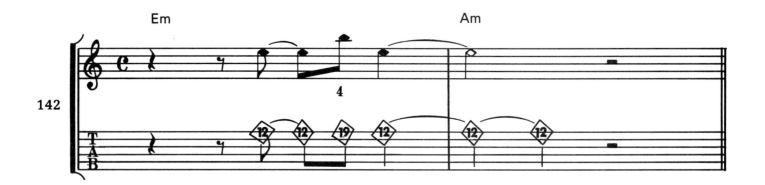

# More Muted Chordal Riffs

Here's a basic Chuck Berry rhythm. Listen to Steve Miller's "Rock'n Me."

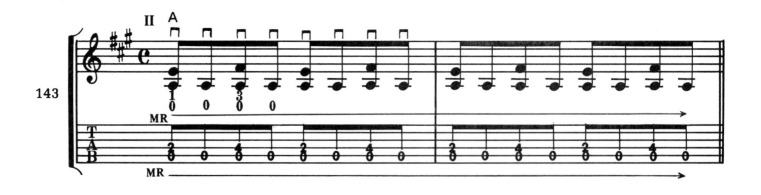

Listen to "All Right Now" by Free. The guitar solo by Paul Kossoff is a gem.

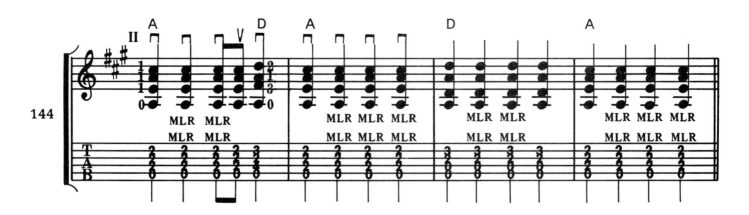

This progression is similar to Frampton's "Show Me the Way."

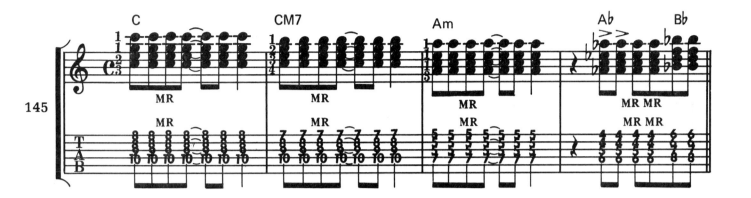

Listen to versions of "I Shot the Sheriff" by either Bob Marley or Eric Clapton.

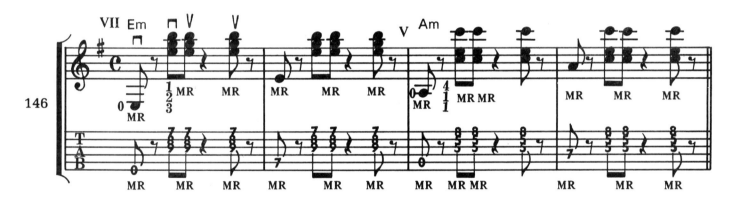

# Diminished and Chromatic Riffs

Listen to the Stray Cats' "Stray Cat Strut" to hear Brian Setzer play something like the following.

This diminished riff (using basically an arpeggiated D°7 chord) appears in similar form on Lou Reed's "Oh Jim."

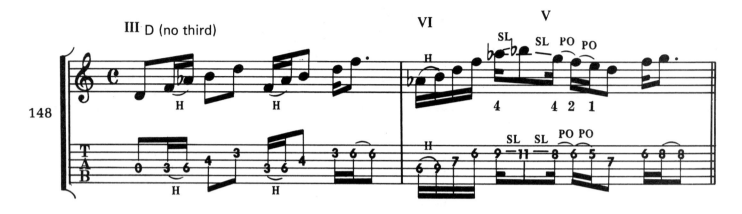

This A diminished riff, played against an A chord, is similar to what is played in Men at Work's "I Like To." It is then played an octave higher.

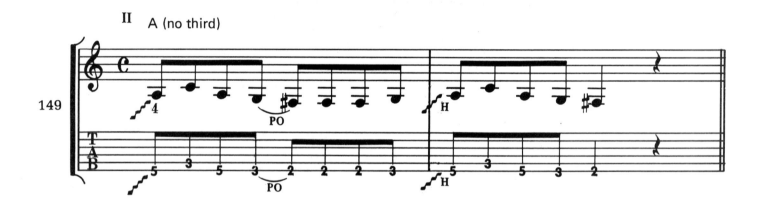

In the following example, the A is bent down chromatically to the G.

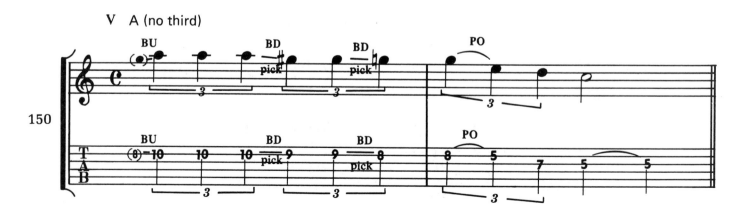

This riff is a perfect example of repeating a motif an octave lower after an initial statement. Check out the Cars' "The Dangerous Type."

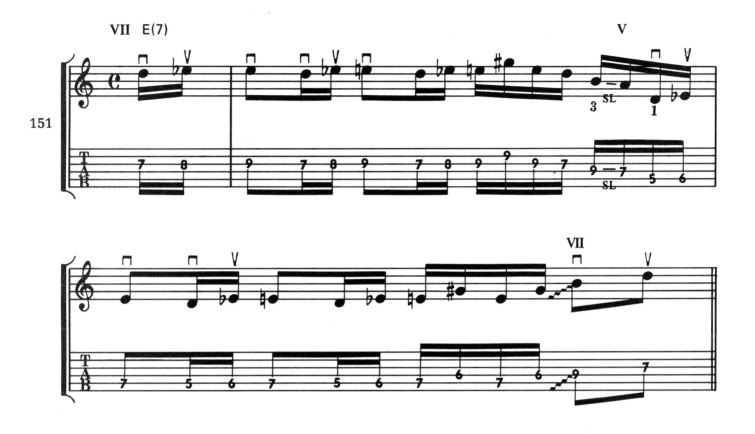

This very effective exposed kickoff is similar to what Mick Jones plays in Foreigner's "Woman in Black." Note how the B is bent up chromatically (in half steps) to the D note over two measures.

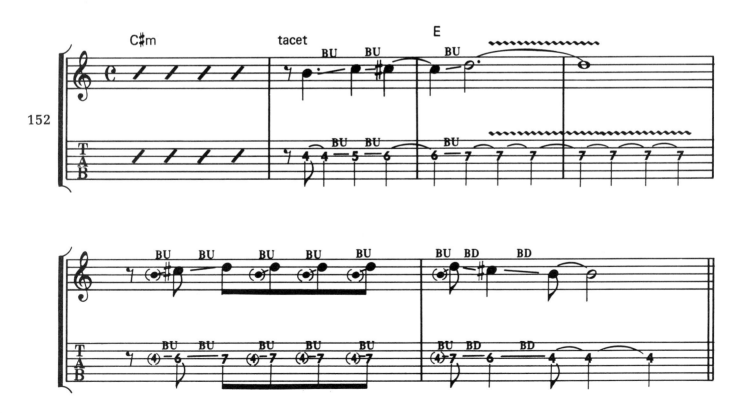

# Advanced Riffs

Listen to Dave Edmunds's "Creature from the Black Lagoon" to hear a riff
like the following one. In the third measure, most of the pulloffs are done
with the fourth finger, so strengthen up!

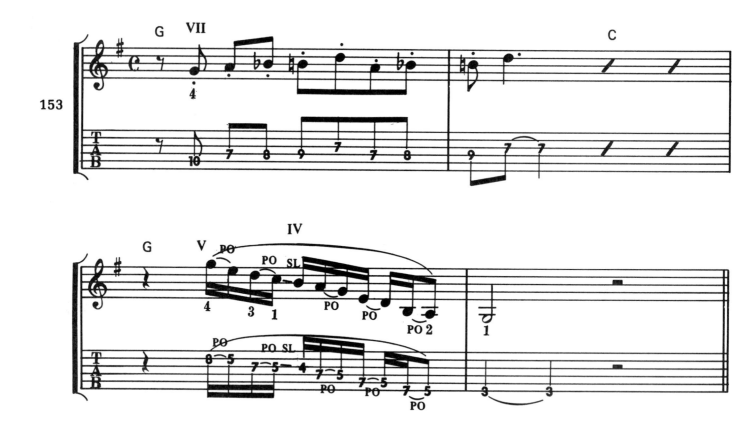

Here's another slide riff which can be played as notated; also similar to a
riff in Elvis's "Waitin' for the End of the World."

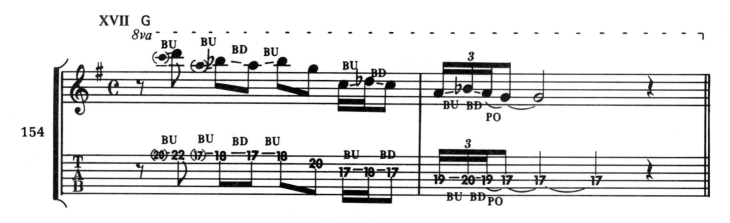

Listen to Wishbone Ash's "Time Was" to hear something like the following.

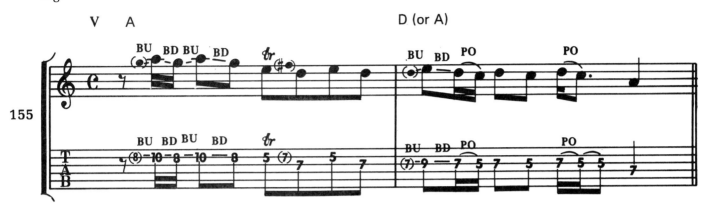

Listen to Steely Dan's "Black Friday" to hear a riff like this one. The first two measures are played off the F♯m (II chord in E) position on the second fret. Use plenty of distortion.

Listen to Mitch Ryder's "Walkin' the Dog" on his first album, *Breakout!* This is a basic accent pattern. Listen to Chuck Berry's "Nadine" and "Maybeline" and T-Rex's "Bang-A-Gong."

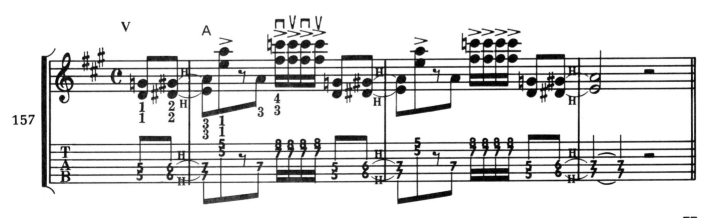

Steve Miller plays a riff like this one during his solo on "Take the Money and Run." Notice that this is written in 'cut time' (¢): two beats to the measure instead of four.

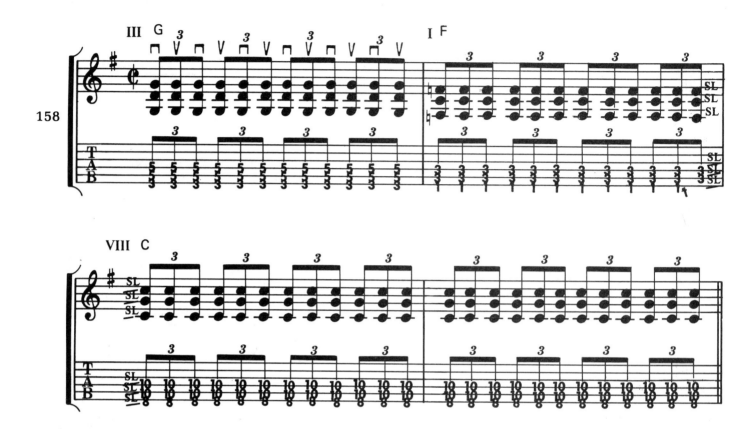

A riff like this one is played in Queen's "Great King Rat." Practice the final bend to make sure that you play it accurately.

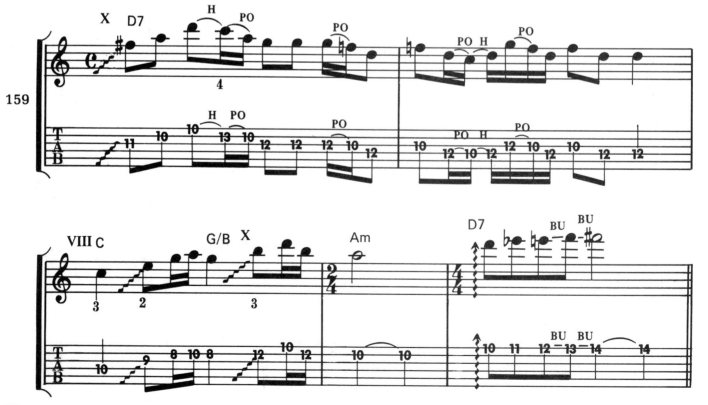

The Cars' Elliot Easton, a great guitarist, plays something just like this on
"You're All I've Got Tonight."

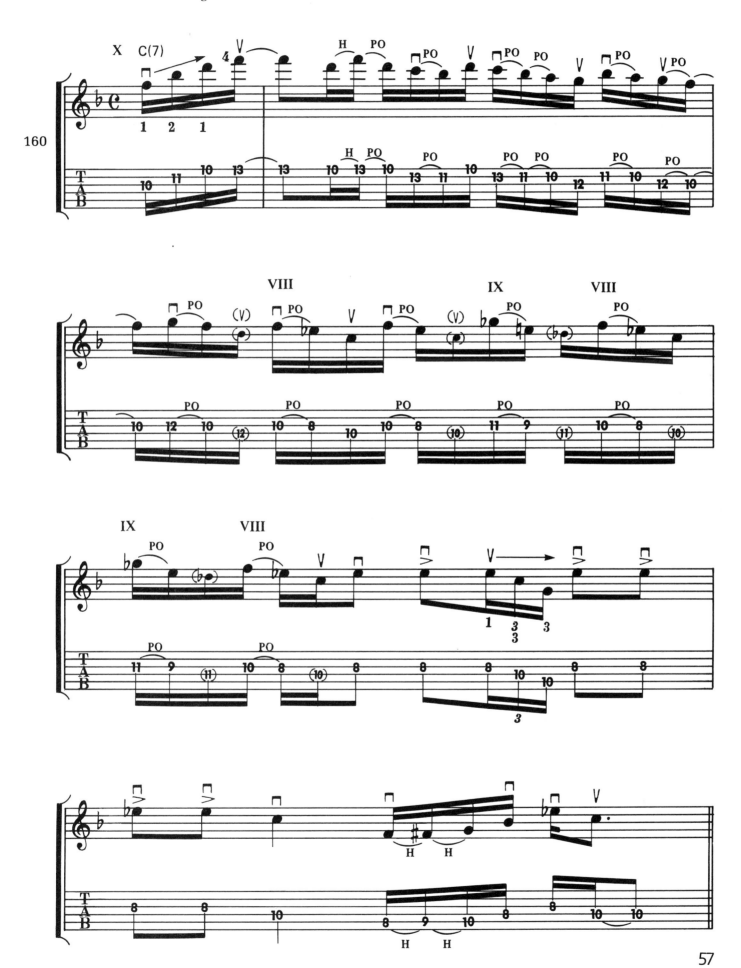

Listen to the amazing two-guitar team of Dick Wagner and Steve Hunter on Lou Reed's "Oh Jim" (on *Lou Reed Live*) to hear a riff like this one.

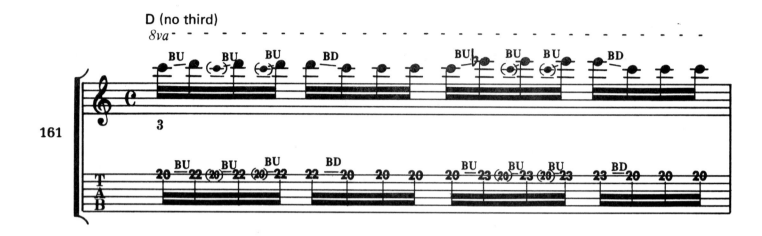

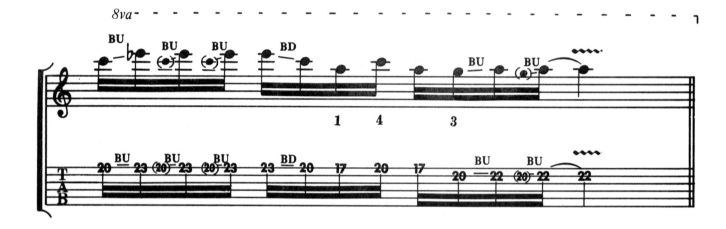

Use your overdrive and you should sound like Elliot Easton of the Cars when you play this riff, which is similar to what he plays in "Since I Held You" on the *Candy-O* album.

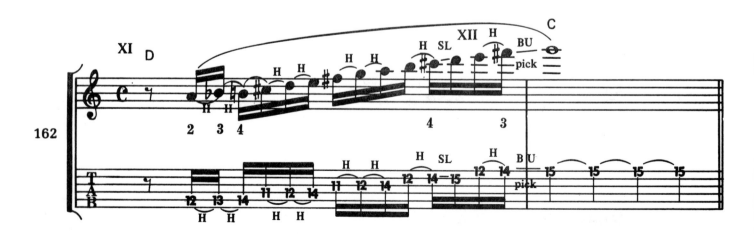

This riff comes from Chuck Berry and is used a lot by Keith Richard and Ron Wood.

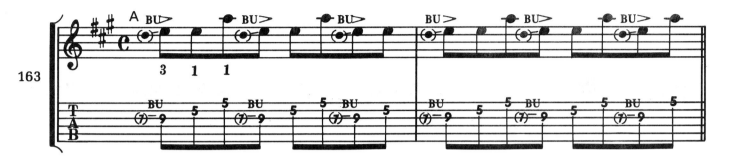

See Chuck Berry's "Johnny B. Goode" and "The Balltrap" and "Wild Side of Life" on Rod Stewart's *A Night on the Town* to hear similar licks.

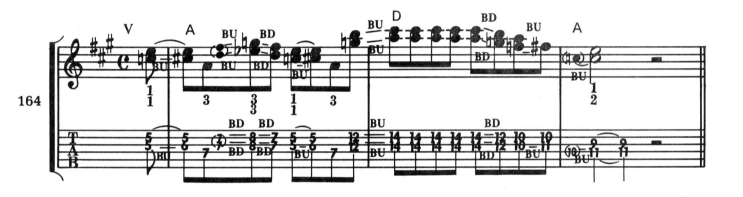

Listen to David Bowie's "Fame" and Jeff Beck's *Blow by Blow* album.

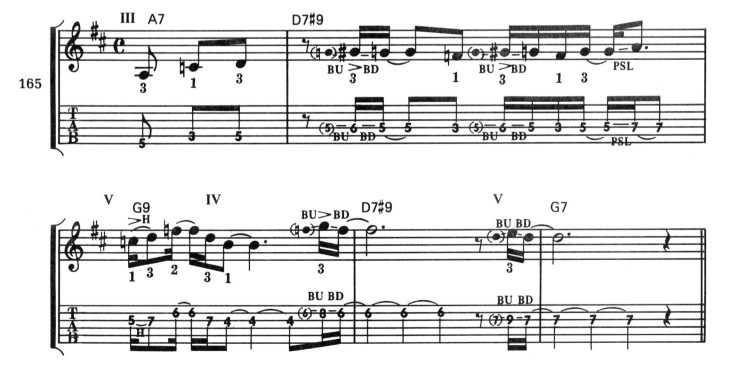

Listen to John Lennon's "What You Got" and Beck's *Wired* album.

# DISCOGRAPHY

| | | |
|---|---|---|
| **Chet Atkins** | Chet Atkins' Workshop | RCA LPM 2232 |
| | Chester and Lester (with Les Paul) | RCA APL1-1167 |
| **Bad Company** | Greatest Hits | Elektra ELK-SE-564 |
| | Bad Company | Swansong SWN 8501 |
| | Desolation Angels | Swansong SWN 8506 |
| **Beatles** | Beatles VI | Capitol T 2358 |
| | Beatles '65 | Capitol ST-2228 |
| | Help! | Capitol MAS 2386 |
| | Revolver | Capitol ST-2576 |
| | Yesterday and Today | Capitol T 2553 |
| | White Album | Capitol SWBO-101 |
| | Sgt. Pepper's Lonely Hearts Club Band | Capitol SMAS-2653 |
| | Let It Be | Capitol SW-11922 |
| **Jeff Beck** | Truth | Epic BN 26413 |
| | Beck-Ola | Epic BN 26478 |
| | Rough and Ready | Epic KE 30973 |
| | Jeff Beck Group | Epic KE 31331 |
| **Chuck Berry** | Chuck Berry's Golden Hits | Mercury 61103 |
| **David Bowie** | The Rise and Fall of Ziggy Stardust | RCA AYL1-3843 |
| **James Burton** | Pieces of the Sky (Emmylou Harris) | Reprise K-2284 |
| | Live Elvis from Memphis to Vegas (Elvis Presley) | RCA LSP-6020 |
| **Paul Butterfield Blues** | First Album | Elektra EKS 7294 |
| **Band (Mike Bloomfield)** | East-West | Elektra EKL 315 |
| **Cars (Elliot Easton)** | The Cars | Elektra GE 135 |
| | Candy-O | Elektra 5E.507 |
| **Cream (Eric Clapton)** | Fresh Cream | ATCO SD 33-206 |
| | Disraeli Gears | ATCO SD 33-232 |
| **Steve Cropper** | Any Otis Redding or Booker T. and the MG's album | |
| **Dire Straits** | Dire Straits (first album) | Warner Bros. K-3266 |
| | Love over Gold | Warner Bros. WRB 1-23728 |
| **Cornell Dupree** | Teasin' | (out-of-print) |
| **Dave Edmunds** | Repeat When Necessary | Swansong SS 8507 |
| **Electric Flag (Mike Bloomfield)** | A Long Time Comin' | Columbia CS-9597 |
| **Elvis Costello** | My Aim Is True | Columbia JC-35037 |
| **Fleetwood Mac** | Mirage | Warner Bros. 23607 |
| | Rumours | Warner Bros. B-3010 |
| | Tusk | Warner Bros. WRB 2 HS-3350 |
| **Foreigner** | Foreigner | Atlantic ATC 19109 |
| | "4" | Atlantic ATC 16999 |
| **Heart** | Dog and Butterfly | Portait PR-35555 |
| | Greatest Hits—Live | Epic KE 2-36888 |

| | | |
|---|---|---|
| **Jimi Hendrix** | Are You Experienced? | Reprise RPS-6261 |
| | Axis: Bold as Love | Reprise RPS-6281 |
| **Ian Hunter** | You're Never Alone | Chrysalis PV-41214 |
| **(Mick Ronson)** | with a Schizophrenic | |
| **Albert King** | King of the Blues Guitar | Atlantic SD 821? |
| | Best of Albert King | Stax 8503 |
| **Freddie King** | Best of Freddie King | MCA 690 |
| | Freddie King Goes | *(out-of-print)* |
| | Surfin' | |
| **Led Zeppelin** | Led Zeppelin I | Atlantic SD-8216 |
| **Lovin' Spoonful** | Best of the Lovin' | Buddah BUD 5706 |
| | Spoonful' | |
| **John Mayall** | John Mayall's | London PS -492 |
| | Bluesbreakers | |
| | (Eric Clapton) | |
| | A Hard Road | London PS-502 |
| | (Peter Green) | |
| **Men At Work** | Cargo | CBS QC 38660 |
| **Steve Miller** | Fly like an Eagle | Capitol SW-11497 |
| **Pretenders** | Pretenders (first album) | Sire 3563 |
| | Pretenders 2 | Sire 3572 |
| **Prince** | Prince | Warner Bros. K-3366 |
| **Lou Reed (Dick Wagner** | Lou Reed | RCA APL 1-0472 |
| **and Steve Hunter)** | Lou Reed Live | RCA APL 1-0959 |
| **Robbie Robertson** | Music from Big Pink | Capitol SKAO-2955 |
| | (The Band) | |
| | John Hammond's So | Vanguard 79178 |
| | Many Roads | |
| **Rolling Stones** | England's Newest Hit- | London PS-375 |
| | makers (first album) | |
| | 12 × 5 | London PS-402 |
| | Out of Our Heads | London PS-429 |
| | The Rolling Stones NOW | London PS-420 |
| | Between the Buttons | London PS-499 |
| | Beggar's Banquet | London PS-539 |
| **Mitch Ryder** | Breakout! | New Voice LP 2002 |
| **(Jimmy McCarty)** | | |
| **Steely Dan** | Katy Lied | ABC ABCD-846 |
| **Rod Stewart** | The Rod Stewart Album | Mercury ML-8001 |
| **(Ron Wood)** | Gasoline Alley | Mercury 1-6264 |
| | Every Picture Tells a | Mercury SRM-1-609 |
| | Story | |
| | Never a Dull Moment | Mercury SRM-1-646 |
| **Stray Cats** | Built for Speed | EMI-America |
| | | ST 17070 |
| **Yardbirds** | For Your Love | Accord SN-7143 |
| | (Beck and Clapton) | |
| | Greatest Hits | Epic FE-38455 |
| **Wishbone Ash** | Argus | MCA 787 |
| **Youngbloods** | The Youngbloods | RCA LSP-3724 |
| **(Jerry Corbitt)** | (first album) | |
| | Earth Music | RCA LSP-3865 |

Stuart Rosner

Mark Michaels

# Riff Cassettes Available!

## by Mark Michaels

## Heavy Metal Riffs for Guitar

Includes riffs in the style of AC/DC (Angus Young), Pat Benatar (Neil Geraldo), Ritchie Blackmore, Foghat, Pink Floyd (David Gilmour), Def Leppard, Iron Maiden, Gary Moore, Judas Priest, Night Ranger, Ozzy Osbourne (Randy Rhoads), REO Speedwagon, Quiet Riot, Rush (Alex Lifeson), Scorpions, Triumph (Rik Emmett) and Van Halen.

## Rockabilly Riffs for Guitar

Includes riffs in the style of The Blasters (Dave Alvin), Bob Wills (Junior Barnard), Bill Haley (Fran Beecher, Danny Cidrone), The Rock and Roll Trio (Paul Burlison), James Burton, Danny Gatton, Gene Vincent (Cliff Gallup), Buddy Holly, Sleepy La Beef, Albert Lee, Grady Martin, Elvis (Scotty Moore), Carl Perkins, Chris Spedding, The Stray Cats (Brian Setzer), Link Wray and more.

## New Wave Riffs for Guitar

Includes riffs in the style of A Flock of Seagulls, Adrian Belew, The Buzzcocks, Robert Fripp, The Psychedelic Furs, Dead Kennedys, Kraut, Television (Richard Lloyd, Tom Verlaine), Roxy Music (Phil Manzanera), The Pretenders, Robert Quine, Squeeze, Billy Idol (Steve Stevens), The Police (Andy Summers), Talking Heads (David Byrne), U2 (The Edge), X (Billy Zoom) and XTC.

## Rock Riffs for Guitar

Includes riffs in the style of Duane Allman, Boston, David Bowie, The Cars, Elvis Costello, Dire Straits, The Eagles, Dave Edmunds, Fleetwood Mac, Foreigner, Peter Frampton, George Harrison, Heart, Jimi Hendrix, Ian Hunter, The Kinks, John Lennon, Bob Marley, Men At Work, Steve Miller, Van Morrison, Jimmy Page, The Pretenders, Prince, Queen, Steely Dan, Leslie West and more.

## Blues Riffs for Guitar

Includes riffs in the style of Jeff Beck, Chuck Berry, Michael Bloomfield, Eric Clapton, Bo Diddley, Peter Green, Buddy Guy, Elmore James, Albert King, B.B. King, Freddie King, Keith Richard, Otis Rush, Kim Simmonds, Mick Taylor and Howlin' Wolf.

- Each companion tape contains *note-for-note* recordings of all the riffs in each book, presented in the *exact order* in which they appear in print.

- Featuring *full band accompaniment* for each riff, not just a single instrument.

- Count-off (1-2-3-4) included for each riff, so you can *play along* and learn faster, more effectively.

--------------------------------------------------------------------

**Yes! I want a Riff Companion. Please send me:**

☐ Heavy Metal Riffs for Guitar Companion Tape   x 9.95 = _____
☐ Rockabilly Riffs for Guitar Companion Tape   x 9.95 = _____
☐ New Wave Riffs for Guitar Companion Tape   x 9.95 = _____
☐ Rock Riffs for Guitar Companion Tape   x 9.95 = _____
☐ Blues Riffs for Guitar Companion Tape   x 9.95 = _____

US Residents: Postage and handling   x 1.50 = _____
Foreign: Postage and handling   x 3.50 = _____
NY Residents add 8¼% sales tax   = _____

Total enclosed   = _____

Send check or Money Order
(US funds only) to:

Riff Companion Series
P.O. Box 1133
Long Island City, NY 11101 USA

Your Name _____
Address _____
City _____ State _____
Country _____ Zip _____

Reader survey (please complete)

I own or have access to
a VCR (videotape player)
  ☐ VHS format
  ☐ Betamax format

Age _____

I read:
☐ Guitar Player
☐ Guitar World
☐ Musician
☐ Rolling Stone
☐ (other) _____